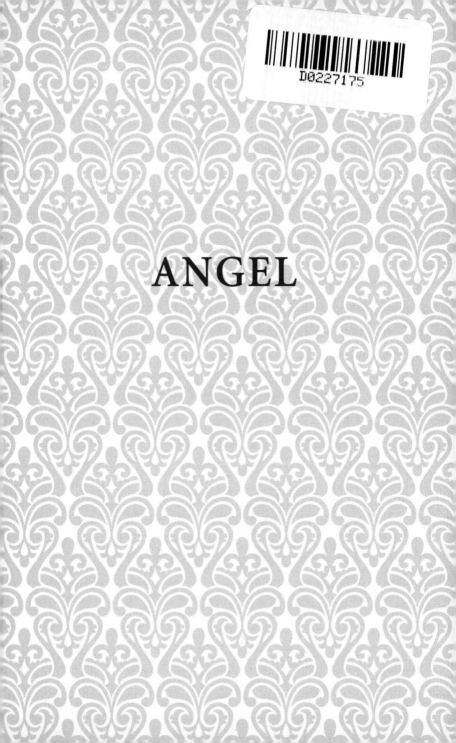

ANGEL

THROUGH MY EYES: NATURAL DISASTER ZONES

Hotaka (Japan)

Shaozhen (China)

Lyla (New Zealand)

Angel (Philippines)

THROUGH MY EYES

Shahana (Kashmir)

Amina (Somalia)

Naveed (Afghanistan)

Emilio (Mexico)

Malini (Sri Lanka)

Zafir (Syria)

THROUGH MY EYES NATURAL DISASTER ZONES

series editor Lyn White

ANGEL

ZOE DANIEL

ALLEN&UNWIN
SYDNEY•MELBOURNE•AUCKLAND•LONDON

First published by Allen & Unwin in 2018

Allen & Unwin
83 Alexander Street
Crows Nest NSW 2065
Australia
Phone: (61 2) 8425 0100
Email: info@allenandunwin.com
Web: www.allenandunwin.com

A catalogue record for this book is available from the National Library of Australia

ISBN 978 1 76011 377 3

For teaching resources, explore
www.allenandunwin.com/resources/for-teachers

Cover and text design by Sandra Nobes
Cover photos: portrait of girl by Juanmonino/iStock;
waves by H3k27/Getty; palm trees by Richard Whitcombe/Alamy;
submerged cars by Jeoffrey Maitem/Getty
Set in 11/15 pt Plantin by Midland Typesetters, Australia
This book was printed in June 2018 by McPherson's Printing Group, Australia.

10 9 8 7 6 5 4 3 2 1

For the people of Tacloban City

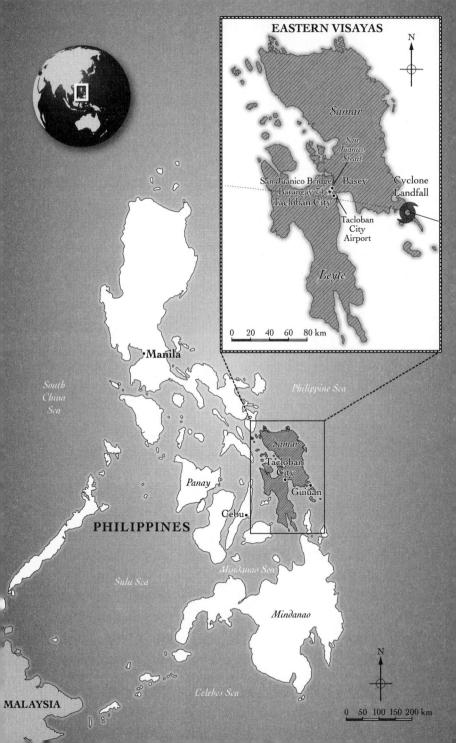

One

Angel and her father are *heading home. They have been fishing all morning and the baskets in the small boat are filled with silvery fish. Angel is perched at the front above the bangka's pointy prow and her father is at the rear, steering the rudder as the outrigger churns through the waves. Juan's normally calm, untroubled face is creased with worry for a storm is coming, and coming fast. The sky is getting darker every second, the wind is up, and rain is beginning to pelt down.*

The little craft hugs the shore and Juan squints. He's trying to make out the distant outline of Tacloban City as they cut through the water, riding wave after wave, each one bigger than the last, but the horizon is obliterated by mist and rain.

Angel, gripping the seat hard to avoid flying out as the boat leaps high, turns, trying to catch her father's eye. He looks through her as if she's not there, scanning the ocean, trying to read the next roll of the waves that threaten to flip them over.

A big black seabird is here too. Angel keeps catching it out of the corner of her eye as it circles, tracking them from a distance, but each time she tries to look at it properly it melts into the mist.

There's a peal of thunder and a flash of lightning. The rain is almost horizontal. Angel's head is full of the roar of the wind. She calls out to her father but the words are blown away before they reach his ears. Again and again she tries to get his attention with her cries.

'Papa! Papa!' It's futile. Juan is entirely focused on the task at hand.

He guns the motor hard, doubling the roar in Angel's ears, and the boat surges forward and up the next mighty wave. It can't be much further, we'll make it home, *Angel thinks. But then, the acceleration suddenly drops away. The little boat hangs, silently suspended on the brink of the wave as if teetering on a cliff.*

'PAPA! HELP ME!'

She screams in terror, and is flung into the sky, the wind carrying her up into the whirling eye of the storm …

Angel wakes with a gasp and is quickly swamped with relief. Her bed is rumpled and cosy and daylight is peeping into the upstairs platform where the family sleeps, but the other beds are empty. Everyone is awake now. Downstairs in the living area, her mother is moving about preparing breakfast. She can hear her twin brothers, Carlo and Cristian, scuffling about teasing each other.

Angel burrows into the bedclothes, her mind still troubled by the nightmare. She often dreams of being on the sea with her father in his sturdy little bangka and she always feels safe and happy when she is with him. Not this time.

For the last few days there have been regular radio reports predicting that a major storm is brewing in the vicinity. A few neighbours have TV sets and yesterday Angel and her father dropped by a friend's house to watch the news bulletins. They saw grim-faced journalists and maps of the Philippines covered in vast, swirling pinwheels. People were arguing: were the reports exaggerated or should they all be heading for the hills? At home later her parents brushed off the warnings. Fierce storms regularly pummel the coastline where they live, but Angel's family is well prepared and they always make it through unscathed. Why should this one be any different?

Angel pushes her uneasiness aside and bounces out of bed. Nothing is going to spoil her special day! She scrambles into her simple school uniform: white shirt, grey and blue tartan skirt and matching tie. Then she runs a brush through the long hair that ripples all the way down her back and draws it into a strong metal clip. This is how she wears it every day. Even though it's beautifully thick and shimmers like black silk she prefers to keep it neatly out of the way. Her best friend Issy sometimes looks at her and sighs, 'What a waste!'

She climbs down the ladder and her mother, Veronica, glances up from the rice cooker and says jokingly, 'Ah, here she is at last. Sleeping in on your birthday. I hope this is not a sign of things to come!'

'Lazy bones! Lazy bones!' chants Cristian from the table where he and Carlo are working their way through bowls of sweet boiled green banana.

Angel smiles. She usually gets up early like her father, before her mother and brothers. She loves the quiet house in the morning as Juan potters about. Sometimes father and daughter sit quietly on the front porch together while Juan sips his scalding, sweet black coffee and plans his day.

'When did Papa leave?' she asks her mother.

'Very early, just after dawn, I think. He's trying out the new motor on the boat and he wants to make sure he gets plenty of fish for tonight.'

Angel feels a thrill of excitement about the birthday feast as she crosses the cool cement floor out onto the porch. The atmosphere is still and muggy and she fills her lungs with the salty air. She barely notices the strong fishy scent that she has lived with all her life. Their house sits just metres from the seawall, with a steep drop to the water, and a clear view across the narrow San Juanico Strait to the island of Samar. Her grandparents live over there on their patch of farmland. She wonders if they have heard the storm warnings. They don't even have a radio. It's a good thing that they're coming to the party tonight and will hear all the news.

The silvery morning sky is streaked with pink – a sign of bad weather – and giant thunderheads are gathering. When she looks to the left, she can see far

4

in the distance the thin line of the San Juanico Bridge snaking across from Leyte on her side of the strait all the way to Samar. To the right, her gaze follows the long curve of the foreshore as it stretches away towards the busy city of Tacloban. She can just see the tower of the Santo Niño church in the centre with its five storeys painted a deep orange colour, and the big storage sheds where the boats unload their fish down on the seashore. Beyond that she can make out the huge white dome of the convention centre. Angel barely remembers the small fishing village that she was born in. Tacloban is now a buzzing capital with shopping centres, government buildings and even a cinema.

Angel scans the shoreline, studded with fishermen's houses just like hers. They make up a colourful mishmash of different shapes and building materials. Some are stronger and sturdier than others, but she suspects most of them are the same inside, small and basic, with a living space downstairs, a sleeping platform upstairs, a narrow roof-space for storage and a porch out the front to catch the breeze.

Her father built their house with his own hands. It's not big or fancy like the new, Western-style villas that are popping up on the hillside overlooking the city. Some of them stand behind high security fences with guards on duty. Her house is simple, but solid, made of timber with a floor of cool, grey cement and a roof of iron built to withstand the seasonal typhoons that cartwheel across the Pacific and through the central Philippines. Next door, the Filipino flag on Mrs Reyes' flagpole hangs limp and still, the proud yellow sun concealed among the drooping red and blue folds.

'Pangaon kita, let's eat!' calls out Veronica. 'Have some breakfast now before these greedy boys wolf down the lot!' The twins are eight years old and it seems to Angel that they never stop eating. Cristian is larger and stockier than Carlo, who is small and slim like his father, but they both have the same huge appetites and seemingly boundless energy.

Before she can move inside, Angel's attention is drawn to a dark shape in the sky overhead, and a black seabird glides into view. The bird swoops in low, almost as if it has its eye on her, and then it turns and flaps away over the water.

Angel shivers.

Come on, Angel. It's just a bird, she tells herself, and with one last glance at the gathering clouds she goes back inside for breakfast.

Two

The radio is on and the announcer is reciting another grim weather forecast. 'No need for that this morning,' says Veronica and she switches to a music station.

As the children eat their eggs and rice, Cristian can't resist teasing his big sister. 'Hey, you're getting old. Soon you'll be a wrinkly little lady like Mrs Reyes!'

Angel just rolls her eyes as the boys shriek with laughter.

'At least when Angel is a wrinkly old lady she will have more teeth than Mrs Reyes!' jokes Carlo.

'That's enough, you two. Have some respect for your elders,' scolds Veronica, who is busy making noodles for the party in the kitchen. It has a wooden table and chairs for dining and a cooking area off to the side with a single tap over a sink. Juan whitewashed the interior walls and Veronica has added little personal touches with colourful pictures of beaches and mountains as well as Bible scenes and a plain wooden cross hanging on the wall.

'Now get going or you will be late for school.' Her voice is sharp but there is a smile on her lips.

'Sorry, Mama. Love you, Mama.' One after the other the boys hug her goodbye.

'Cheeky scoundrels,' she calls after them. 'Be good!'

Angel kisses her mother and Veronica regards her daughter approvingly.

'Have I told you how much like your father you are?' she says.

Angel smiles. Her mother has told her, many times, and Angel never tires of hearing it.

Veronica returns the smile and waves her tea towel at Angel. 'Have a wonderful day, birthday girl.'

Angel walks along the busy Pan-Philippine highway towards Tacloban with the boys skipping in front. Up ahead the dark thunderclouds are blotting out parts of the sky. It's only 7 a.m., but the air is already stifling. All that moisture means there is plenty of lush green vegetation around. People say all you have to do is poke a plain old stick into the ground and a day later it will have sprouted leaves!

The children pick their way down the busy footpath leading into the city. The roadside is jammed with stores selling fruit and snacks, motor oil and plastic containers, and the road itself is seething with cars, motorbikes and jeepneys.

Tacloban is divided into more than a hundred barangays and Angel's family lives in Barangay 74.

After about ten minutes they reach Angel's old elementary school in Barangay 6, where she leaves the boys at the gate.

'See you here at three-thirty,' she calls after them as they disappear inside the drab grey building. They will eat their school lunch of rice, meat or fish and gravy in their classroom. It's a long day, but they have been coming here since they were five years old and are used to it.

Angel keeps walking along the busy road for another ten minutes to her junior high school. She is in her first year and she is determined to study hard so that she can graduate from high school and go on to college. She is good at all the basic subjects at school like Maths, Science, English and Philippine literature, but Social Science is her favourite subject, and she is looking forward to that afternoon's geography lesson.

'Angel! Angel! Wait up!'

She turns around and there's Issy, her best friend, running up with her brother, Justin, behind her. 'Happy birthday to you!' Issy chants, grabbing Angel by the hand. 'Now we are both teenagers – woo-hoo!'

Issy and Angel have known each other forever. Their mothers have been good friends ever since they were both newlyweds and sang in the church choir together. Issy's father also started out as a fisherman like Juan, but some years ago he opened a market stall and now he makes a very decent living selling fish that other people catch. The two families often go to church and socialise together.

Issy and Angel are devoted friends but they are also different in many ways: while Angel is quiet and serious, Issy is loud and playful. She loves make-up and following all the latest fashions and music trends. Today her shoulder-length hair is coiled up into an elaborate plait and she has hot-pink studs twinkling in her ears. Her warm, infectious smile draws people to her and she is well liked and loves to be sociable.

'I can't wait for the party tonight. I've been praying for the storm to hold off until tomorrow. Justin has too, haven't you, kuya?'

Issy's big brother is fifteen and in his first year of high school. He acts like he is annoyed by his chatty, popular little sister but he is secretly very proud and protective of her and diligently walks her to and from school every day. A full head taller than the girls, he flicks his long fringe to the side and peers down at Angel.

'Good luck being a teenager, pipsqueak,' he says sarcastically, 'you're going to need it.' And he strides off. Angel frowns after him. She just doesn't get Justin; he always seems to be as grumpy as Issy is cheerful. She wishes he'd stop treating her like a silly little girl.

'Don't mind him,' says Issy. 'He's got to study for a big maths test tomorrow so no partying for him.' Angel knows Issy thinks that she and Justin are very similar – both serious, sensible, and highly motivated – and hopes that one day they will stop being at loggerheads.

The two girls link arms and chat excitedly the rest of the way to school. Even though the plain boxy building was painted bright green a few years ago, it is already faded and grubby again. Inside, the students are restless, most of them fidgeting in the heat, wondering when the storm will hit and whether it will be bad enough for them to be sent home early. The lessons are mostly taught in English, but sometimes in Filipino and even a bit of Waray-waray, which is their regional language.

As the morning wears on, Angel keeps watch out the window. Storm clouds pile up over the city and sharp gusts of wind tip motos onto their sides and send plastic bags and pieces of loose litter twisting into the sky.

The rain begins bucketing down and the teacher covers the classroom windows with long wooden blinds, tying them down at the bottom to strong metal bolts. There's no real need for glass in the windows in such a warm climate, except when the rain turns horizontal and pelts in, damaging their few precious books and leaving big puddles on the cement floor.

The day seems to drag on forever. Even the geography lesson seems dull and boring as the rain pours steadily outside. At last it's three-fifteen and the students burst out of the classrooms. Luckily, the rain has stopped and Angel hurries to collect her brothers. On their way home the boys cavort in the wind, skipping and spinning, chasing the flying leaves and litter kicked up by the gusts.

'Hurry up, you two, we have to get home before the rain comes back.'

Carlo and Cristian laugh and tease her, running around her in circles. They're so glad to be free after being cooped up inside all day. When she finally gets to the house, Angel sees her father's bangka securely tethered but fighting the ropes as the wind and swell push it up and down on the heavy wash of the waves. The old taklub basket Juan uses to catch fish is swinging wildly from the mooring post and she runs to untie it before it's torn away into the gale. A deafening thunder-clap booms overhead and the sky opens. A few heavy drops soon become a teeming downpour and Angel ducks into the house, completely drenched.

Her mother is at the timber table, filleting piles of fish.

'Is Papa still at the market?' Angel asks.

'Yes he is. It was a good catch today so as soon as he got home he went straight there.'

At that moment Juan comes in the door behind her, shedding a dripping raincoat as he goes.

'Hello, birthday girl!'

'Papa! How was the market?'

'We sold out of everything, but I kept plenty of fish for the party,' he says happily.

Angel's father is not a big man – only about a head taller than her – but he is lean and agile and very strong. He could pass for much younger than his forty-odd years, if it wasn't for the vivid white streak that flares up from the side-part in his thick black hair. He jokes that it gives him an air of wisdom and authority.

Angel reaches for a towel and quickly pats herself dry so that she can start helping her mother.

Juan places his hand lightly on her shoulder. 'I have something to give to you.' The boys crowd around as he extracts a small box from his pocket and hands it to his daughter.

Generally, birthdays don't involve extravagant presents in their family, but Angel is turning thirteen, and Juan has been saving this gift for a long time. Veronica dries her hands on a cloth and moves over to stand by her husband.

For a moment, the family is silent, and the only sound is the rain pounding the roof. They all wait expectantly for Angel to open her present. She turns the tattered little box over in her hands. It looks old. It's made of faded jade-green paper, tied with a frayed golden ribbon.

She looks at her parents, unsure.

'Open it,' urges her father softly.

Obediently Angel unties the ribbon and lays it carefully on the kitchen table. She slowly opens the lid. Inside, nestled on a piece of soft, white cotton, is a single, silvery pearl on a sturdy golden chain.

'I saved every month from my work on the cargo ships, and bought that pearl for your mother as a wedding gift,' Juan tells her. 'But she asked me to give it to our firstborn daughter instead. She said, "Save it for the day when she is old enough to take care of it." I have carried it with me ever since and now it's that time.'

Angel has never seen anything so beautiful or owned something so valuable.

'Oh, Papa.'

'Wear it always, my Angel, and you will know that I am with you.'

Three

The rain has stopped and the clouds are slinking away across the evening sky.

'Only a rainstorm after all,' says Angel, relieved. She is outside with her father, helping to string the rainbow party lights along the roofline.

'There she is!' someone shouts and the two of them turn around.

Staggering down the road is a tall skinny man with a shock of white hair and a short plump woman in a bright headscarf. The elderly couple is laden with plastic bags and all smiles. Angel runs to her grandpa, Pedro, and reaches up to kiss him on the cheek. Then she hugs her grandma, Gloria, and takes the bags that are weighing her down.

'Look at this young lady,' chuckles Pedro. 'I swear she is three inches taller.'

'Thank you, dear,' says Gloria, shaking her cramped arms. Despite their advancing years, Pedro and Gloria are very healthy for their age. A lifetime working the farm has made them strong and fit.

Inside, Veronica fusses around her parents, drawing up chairs and bringing them cups of tea. Their farm on the island of Samar is only about forty kilometres away, but travelling the rough, bumpy roads by jeepney can take a couple of hours, especially in heavy traffic. Before the San Juanico Bridge was built they would cross the strait by boat. The sea was far less reliable, but on a good day the journey would take half the time. Now they have to travel all the way up to the bridge, cross the two-kilometre span, which is usually bumper to bumper with jeepneys, cars and motos, and then catch another bone-jarring jeepney all the way down to Barangay 74. It's a sweaty, cramped journey at the best of times, but quite an ordeal at their age.

Angel is opening the plastic bags and marvelling at the variety of food that Gloria and Pedro have brought with them. Her mouth waters as the delicious smell of baduya nga pasayan wafts up. Angel loves her grandmother's shrimp fritters and is excited to see that she has also made lumpia rolls and light, buttery corioso cookies. The family's wooden table is crammed with dishes for the guests to help themselves to. There are platters of fresh fried fish and shrimps and bowls of pancit, with delicious morsels of chicken and seafood peeking out among the slippery noodles. In the centre is a mountain of fragrant rice with crunchy vegetables, a pile of fried chicken and Gloria's spicy lumpia rolls. Afterwards, Veronica will put out plates of sweet taro pudding.

'What a feast!' exclaims Cristian and he manages to snatch a lumpia before Veronica can shoo him away.

'Maupay nga gab-i, good evening. Any room on that table for more?' Their neighbour, Mrs Reyes, stands in the doorway holding a plate of fried bananas sprinkled with sugar.

'Maupay nga gab-i to you, Mrs Reyes. Let me help you with that,' says Veronica. She takes the plate and sniffs appreciatively. 'Marasa, salamat! Delicious, thank you!'

'Waray sapayan, you're welcome,' says Mrs Reyes and smiles at the compliment. She is a tiny woman with twinkly brown eyes and a small round bun permanently fixed on the top of her head, like a bread roll. No one knows exactly how old she is, but it seems like she has always been in the neighbourhood. She can often be heard singing along to the radio at the top of her crackly voice and she wears brightly coloured shirts and baggy knickerbocker shorts tied at the knee. The children giggle at her antics; once she chomped her way through a whole fried chicken even though she has lost almost all of her teeth! But Veronica won't hear a word said against her. 'She's just lonely. Her husband died years ago and her children all left to work in the city and on the cruise boats. She scarcely ever gets to see her grandchildren.'

Mrs Reyes is a good friend and neighbour and the family includes her in all its celebrations and activities. Sometimes Juan helps her fix things around the house, but she is fiercely independent and proud that she is still so self-sufficient.

'Pedro and Gloria! How lovely to see you on this happy day. You are very brave to take a chance on the weather,' observes Mrs Reyes.

'We wouldn't miss this birthday for the world,' replies Pedro. 'It's not every day your beloved granddaughter leaves her childhood behind.'

Angel ducks her head shyly.

'Don't worry about us. We will leave for Samar first thing tomorrow and be home in plenty of time!' says Gloria.

A young man with spiky gelled hair, beefy arms and a huge grin comes in lugging an impressive karaoke machine.

'Where shall I set this up?' he booms.

'Sebastian!' shout Cristian and Carlo together.

Juan has arranged for their neighbour to play music at the party. Sebastian works as a fisherman to support his wife and baby son, but he loves pop music and enjoys DJ'ing for a small price at local celebrations. It's a wonderful surprise for Angel and her friends, who love to sing and dance.

A few minutes later Issy arrives and at the sight of the microphones and flashing lights she claps her hands in delight. 'Woo-hoo! Let's get this party started!'

'Just a moment,' announces Veronica firmly. 'Before we begin the festivities, let us give thanks for all the good things that we have here tonight.' Obediently, everyone bows their heads and Veronica utters a short prayer.

Her eyes tightly closed, Angel reaches up and lightly

touches the pearl around her neck. Her lips curl into a smile of pure happiness.

When they arrive at school the next day, Angel and Issy are full of chatter about what a great party it was. The little house was bursting with friends and neighbours and there was plenty of food for all. The best part, though, was the karaoke.

'Sebastian is such a good DJ!' says Issy.

'And he's got great moves too. He can really dance,' says Angel.

'Hey, I didn't know Carlo had a good voice!' says Issy.

'I know,' replies Angel. 'He's always singing. He wants to be a popstar like Jireh Lim. Not so good with the words though.' They laugh, remembering Carlo making up his own lyrics when the ones on the screen flashed by too fast for him.

'What about you?' says Angel. 'You did a great version of that Katy Perry song.'

'Ha!' laughs Issy. 'It was only good because Mrs Reyes joined in at the end!' And together the girls roar the chorus.

When they finally control their giggles, Issy asks quietly, 'Are you wearing it today?'

Angel glances around at the other students streaming by and turning her back on them she carefully lifts out the pearl on the chain that has been concealed beneath her school shirt.

'A real Filipino pearl,' sighs Issy. 'It's beautiful.'

Angel smiles proudly as she tucks it back out of sight. She won't be showing it off very often; it's too precious.

'I better go. I need to finish that homework,' says Angel. 'I didn't get a chance to do it last night and I'm worried that Mrs Fernandez might spring a test on us.'

'Oh come on, Angel,' scoffs Issy. 'You'd breeze through a test even if you hadn't done the reading. And look, here's Nadia and Jasmine...'

Angel waves as the other girls approach. 'Catch you later,' she calls as she heads into the school building. There's still time before the bell rings and Angel enters the quiet classroom and takes a seat at the back.

The cane blinds are up and there's a breeze wafting through the barred windows, ruffling the papers of her maths book. Angel hears the heels of her teacher, Mrs Fernandez, clicking in the concrete hallway as she approaches the classroom. Mrs Fernandez pauses to say hello to Mr Mercado, who teaches in the classroom next door, and Angel can hear the pair talking quietly. Their urgent tone makes her tilt her head and shuffle a bit closer to the open window.

'There were back-to-back bulletins on TV this morning,' Mr Mercado says. 'Sounds really bad. Overseas they're calling it Typhoon Haiyan instead of Yolanda.'

Mrs Fernandez sighs, 'Yolanda is far too pretty a name for a storm.'

Mr Mercado grunts in agreement. 'Well, the storm with the pretty name is headed this way. We will have to close the school and the government wants everyone to evacuate. Above all, we must try not to worry the children. They say it's a super storm.'

Mrs Fernandez scoffs at that. '"Super storm"? That sounds like something made up by the cable news channels to me!'

Mr Mercado laughs.

Angel leans away from the window and presses her back against the cool, damp wall of the classroom. Another storm, and a super storm at that. *What's a 'super storm' anyway? We have typhoons every year, how bad can it be?*

As Mrs Fernandez comes in followed by Angel's classmates, Angel looks out the window and up at the heavy, grey sky. *Where are you, Yolanda? What have you got in store for us?*

At lunch break Angel tells her friends what she heard the teachers say about the storm.

Nadia's father drives a jeepney and she says the storms are good business for him because of all the people rushing to evacuate. On the other hand, Jasmine says that this morning after they heard the reports, her father announced they would be going to stay with his sister's family, who live further inland.

'We are going to leave first thing in the morning so no more school for the rest of the week!'

'Is that your aunty with the big television?' asks Issy.

'Two televisions and only one kid!' sighs Jasmine, who has five noisy brothers and sisters and no television. 'I love staying with them!'

Issy doesn't know yet what her parents are planning, but Angel knows what her family will do.

'My mum will go and stay with my grandparents at the farm. She worries about them. I think she should take the boys this time, too.'

'What about you?' asks Nadia. 'Don't you feel a bit scared with your house right on the seafront?'

'Papa and I will stay here to take care of things. We're a good team!'

'Angel, look!' Issy is pointing behind her and Angel turns to see her mother hurrying towards her with Carlo and Cristian close behind.

'What are you doing here, Mama? School hasn't finished yet!'

'That storm we heard was coming? It's a big one and we need to get ready. I thought I'd pick you and the boys up early. I've told Mrs Fernandez.' Veronica smiles at her daughter's friends. 'Don't worry though, girls.'

She puts an arm around Issy and gives her a reassuring squeeze. 'Everything will be okay. We're used to big storms around here, aren't we?'

Angel hugs her friends. It's strange to be leaving school before lessons are finished. 'I'll see you in a few days when this is all over...'

Four

Outside the school Veronica flags down a bright-green jeepney bus and the four of them climb aboard. They squeeze together on the hard seats, sweating freely as they cram in skin-on-skin with the other passengers. The boys grip the window bars tightly as the jeepney weaves through bikes and motos and cars. The air is filled with the sound of honking and beeping and the acrid stench of hundreds of vehicle exhausts alongside the occasional whiff of freshly peeled fruit at a roadside stall.

The city streets are full of buildings jammed together higgledy-piggledy. Then the scene opens up as they pass the town hall with wide green lawns flanking the stairway leading up to its grand square entrance. Angel imagines it is cool and spacious inside and everyone speaks in hushed tones as they conduct their important business.

The four of them clamber off the jeepney at the street corner where the Santo Niño church with its tall steeple and orange walls has towered proudly over the ever-expanding town for almost 175 years. The church is surrounded by carefully tended gardens, and the sweet scent of dozens of frangipani trees fills the air.

Even though the children have been to Santo Niño countless times, they are always slightly awestruck when they walk through the wide entrance doors. The interior has a calm serenity about it, with its stone-tiled floors, long, polished timber pews and soaring ceilings. It's a welcome escape from the frenetic traffic and the heat outside. The three children sit on a pew near the front, quietly gazing up at the stained-glass windows, their saintly occupants brightly backlit by shafts of afternoon sun.

Veronica and the children aren't the only ones who've come to church on this weekday afternoon. Many members of the congregation have gathered to discuss the incoming storm and to glean whatever information they can from their friends, and from the Catholic priest.

Father Jose is at the front of the church, robed in white, calmly explaining the situation to the throng of parishioners. He has been at the church for more than ten years and is much loved by his loyal flock. He wears very thick glasses and they make his kind brown eyes even larger as he peers at the worried faces before him.

'Yes, I'm afraid that it is very serious. They're saying it may be the strongest storm the world has ever seen,' he tells one. 'You must prepare as best you can,' he tells another. 'The government is recommending that you secure your valuables and move to high ground. There are schools and churches and community halls where you will be safe.'

Veronica has been coming to Santo Niño since she moved from Samar to Leyte to marry Juan. As an active member of the church she knows Father Jose very well. Angel watches as her mother pushes her way to the front. The priest beckons her forward and puts his cool, dry hands over hers. 'You must make plans to keep all your children safe, Veronica,' Angel overhears him telling her mother gently. 'Are you going to go to your parents again? I know it is inconvenient, but I think that everyone should be moving away from the coast. Perhaps you should take all the children. This one is not like previous typhoons.'

Angel listens intently from where she sits in the pew, while the boys wander off to chase a small bird that's doing a loop-the-loop through the church's cavernous arches.

'When will it come, Father?' Veronica is speaking quietly but Angel can still make out her question from where she sits silently on the hard wooden seat.

'They are telling us it will make landfall in two days' time, on Friday morning, early.' Father Jose shifts his gaze to Angel and meets her eyes across the crowd. 'Tell Juan there is room here if he and the children need it. Now I must prepare to shelter our people. There is a great deal to do.'

He pats Veronica's hand and turns, his long robes swirling across the tiled floor as he exits the church through an arched doorway into the back garden.

Veronica sits down next to Angel, the two of them savouring a moment of quiet. Angel watches as her mother tucks the two wings of her chin-length bob behind her ears; her pretty, heart-shaped face is creased with worry. Angel can imagine the thoughts racing through her mind. Should the family evacuate from their home? What if people steal their few precious belongings while they are away? Where should they take the children?

Angel knows her mother is worrying about Gloria and Pedro, too. They are frail. They won't be able to weather such a storm on their own and Veronica's brother lives too far away in Malaysia to be of any help. Veronica sighs heavily.

Angel understands that her mother is worried about what might happen in Tacloban, but she knows that she and her father could evacuate with the boys while their mother is away. They could take a few basic items from the house and move to the church, or even the convention centre on the way to the airport. It's quite a distance to get there, but it's solid and strong so they should be safe. She doesn't like the idea of leaving their home unprotected though. Her father has worked his whole life for all that they have.

'We better get prepared, Mama,' she says, turning to Veronica. 'You should pack and go to Samar. Grandma and Grandpa will be waiting for you – they need your help. Papa and the boys and I will make the house ready for the storm.'

She stands and straightens her school skirt. 'Our home will weather this typhoon, just as it always has before.'

Veronica regards her daughter appraisingly. Drawing her into a quick embrace, she whispers into her ear: 'I am so very proud of you.' Together they follow the boys, who have chased the little bird out the front doors of the church. The tiny creature soars on a light breeze across the street and heads towards the sea, which shimmers flat and glassy in the distance. It's hard to believe a storm will soon be here, let alone a super storm.

The four of them walk to the nearby market to pick up some supplies before catching another jeepney home. Veronica purchases some rice, some cooking oil and a few vegetables. She has been salting and drying their extra fish so there will be enough to keep them fed for a while. There's not much left to buy at the market anyway. It's been busy with people stocking up before they bunker down.

Many of the stallholders are preparing to shut their businesses. As they sell the last of what they have, they pack up their trestle tables, stacking them on top of each other inside the few covered shops. Pots and pans and cooking utensils are boxed and piled on top. Shop fronts are covered with bamboo blinds and sheets of plastic, gaps are taped to keep out rain, loose corners are nailed down to prevent them being caught by the wind. Shopkeepers who live inside leave a single flap undone, so they can enter and exit until they finally lock themselves in against the onslaught.

Angel takes comfort from the fact that in spite of the government's warnings to move, not everyone is evacuating. Perhaps they haven't heard the radio and

TV broadcasts or they've ignored them. Either way, they've decided not to go. They are going about their storm preparations as usual with an air of methodical routine.

In the jeepney on the way home Angel watches more people packing their belongings. Shops and houses have been shuttered with blinds or sheets of tarp and plastic. Bricks and bags of rice have been placed on tin roofs to keep them from flying off in the wind. Anything that can be tied down has been lashed to something else that's solid. Cars have been covered in makeshift boxes of cardboard and packing tape. Those on the move have all their valuables with them, packed in cheap striped plastic bags with handles. Passing jeepneys are full, their roofs stacked high with bags and baskets. *Nadia's father will be doing good business*, she thinks to herself.

It's getting dark when they arrive home, but Angel and her mother immediately begin their well-known routine. Veronica fills some jugs and bottles with water from their single tap. She gathers rice and other food supplies and puts them in sturdy woven bags to take to her parents. Then she bundles up a few blankets and towels and some soap, along with matches and a couple of candle stubs and finally a change of clothes for herself.

Together, mother and daughter pack all of the family's clothes and linens inside plastic bags in a couple of crates. The remaining food and water is placed in another. Angel climbs the wooden ladder into the roof-space and hauls the crates up with the boys helping her from below. She hangs all of the cooking utensils on nails high on the walls. Anything else she puts in bags, which she hangs wherever she can. The storm will bring strong winds, but the bigger threat to their possessions may be flooding from the sea.

Angel takes some candles and matches and puts them on a ledge where they can be found in the dark.

'Just in case,' she mutters to herself.

Late into the night Angel can hear her parents talking downstairs. They decide that the boys will go with Veronica because they will be safer inland at the farm. Angel smiles to herself, cosy and warm in her bed, when they agree that she can stay behind to help protect the family's things and keep her father company.

The next morning everyone is up early. Angel sees Juan head out to secure his boat and help the neighbours do the same. She knows his fellow fishermen will have brought their boats in one by one, tying them close to the shoreline in protected areas or dragging them up onto the land to keep them safe. It's hard and exhausting work.

Even though the trip to Samar usually only takes a couple of hours, Veronica is eager to get going. Many other people are also on the move as they try to beat the storm so the going will be slow. Veronica and the boys will take a jeepney to the bridge and cross between the two islands, but it won't take them all the way to her parents' house. They will have to hitch a ride on the other side.

Angel's father stops for a moment outside their house and says his farewell to Veronica and the boys.

'The forecast is very grim, but you have the whole day to get there. I will feel better with you three safe at the farm.' He hands his wife one of the family's two old mobile phones, sealed tight in the waterproof bag that he uses when he takes it out fishing. The reception on Samar is not very good, so he tells her to phone him when she can, just to let him know that she and the boys are okay. He's added a couple of hundred pesos' worth of credit to make sure she can get in touch.

'Go now!' He hugs his wife and sons hard. Veronica clasps his hands between hers and closes her eyes for a moment in what Angel knows is a silent prayer.

'I will be back before dark,' Juan tells Angel as he heads out again.

Last thing, Veronica and Angel go next door to see Mrs Reyes. The elderly widow is coming down her ladder after packing things away in the roof-space.

'You shouldn't be up there, Mrs Reyes. Let me help you!' says Veronica.

'I'm up and down ladders all the time, my dear. To tell you the truth, I feel safer up there than down here,' she chuckles.

Laying her hand gently on the younger woman's arm she asks, 'Are you sure you have time to make the journey before the storm? There is a strange feeling in the air – I don't like it.'

'We've got the whole day,' Veronica replies. 'The storm isn't due until tomorrow.'

Mrs Reyes shakes her head and continues to bustle about, stacking pots and pans into a plastic tub and packing a bag of rice and a jar of boiled banana into a mesh sack. Angel helps where she can.

Veronica takes the tub and places it on top of a wooden cabinet against the wall of the little hut. Mrs Reyes' house is tiny but cheerful in spite of its scuffed linoleum floor and flaking paintwork. Angel remembers years ago, it was painted a vivid sea green by one of her two sons, but it's now faded to a kind of aquamarine. There are photographs of her children and grandchildren pinned to the wall alongside colourful crayon drawings. Outside, the faded Filipino flag flutters in the rising breeze.

'I would leave myself,' Mrs Reyes says, 'but I'm worried someone might break in and steal my things... not that there's much to take!'

Veronica smiles.

'Argh, I'm too old to run away from storms. We'll watch out for each other, won't we?' Mrs Reyes says to Angel. She turns to Veronica. 'Now you keep yourself safe, my dear, and those cheeky boys of yours. Okay?'

Veronica nods silently. She is clearly in turmoil as she and Angel walk back to the house. 'Perhaps you should all come with me,' she says. 'It doesn't feel right to leave you, Angel.'

Already, the wind is strengthening and they both know the travellers must get on the road. The traffic is bound to be terrible, and they must reach their destination before dark. Their eyes are drawn to the heavy clouds and the dark, choppy waves.

In the end it's Angel who speaks first. 'Go now and take the boys, it's what you agreed. I will stay and look after the house with Papa. He will be back before dark and expect to find me here.'

Veronica begins to protest, but Angel has taken control now. She brings the luggage outside the house and hands her brothers a bag each to carry and some boiled sweets that she has been saving.

'You must go,' she tells her mother. 'Look at the sky.'

The clouds have that green tinge that comes with very heavy rain. They've all seen it before.

Reluctantly, Veronica picks up her things. 'We'll be back as soon as the storm is over,' she says.

'You take care of Mama,' says Angel to her brothers.

For once they are subdued and solemn.

'She is safe with me,' says Cristian with confidence. 'And me,' smiles Carlo bravely. 'I will keep my eye on both of them.'

Angel watches her mother and brothers walk to the end of the lane. She can hear the boys' young voices: 'When are we going to see Papa and Angel again?' 'How long do we have to stay in Samar?' 'Ouch! My sandal is pinching me already...' The three of them turn together and wave, and then they're gone.

Suddenly Angel feels very tired and she plonks down on the step. The wind is rising and it's starting to rain, but for the moment she just sits and stares around her, twisting her fingers in the twine from the old taklub that is tied securely to the mooring post beside her.

Everywhere is frantic activity as people make their final preparations. Normally everyone in the neighbourhood helps each other when a storm is coming, but now there simply isn't time and it's everyone for themselves: shifting valuables inside, securing possessions as high from the ground as possible, hammering and tying things down.

A dark shape is hopping about in one of the fishing boats drawn up from the water. Angel realises it's a large seabird – maybe even the same one that she spotted on the morning of her birthday. One of the fishermen must have left some of his catch in the boat and now the bird is gulping down all the scraps. *Surely it can't be that hungry*, Angel thinks, and then she remembers Juan telling her once that birds are known to eat as much as possible when bad weather is coming. Somehow they know to store as much nourishment as they can because their access to food might be severely disrupted in the coming days.

While she watches, the bird spreads its wings and lifts into the air, beating strongly against the buffeting wind. And then just like the other day, it dives towards Angel and circles above her before turning inland and flapping away.

This time, she feels a bit annoyed. 'Why are you picking on me?' she mutters. 'Is it because you can escape while I'm stuck here?' How she wishes her whole family could fly away and find somewhere safe until it's all over.

Five

Angel spends the rest of the day cleaning up and preparing the house. She ties down everything possible and carefully places thick sheets of cardboard over the windows using plenty of tape to secure them. Last thing she clambers upstairs and checks the roof for holes. It looks good.

When Juan returns home at dusk they eat some cold rice and dried fish and then finish barricading the little house, bracing the door with the table and chairs. Angel wears her shorts and shirt to bed, assuming she'll have to get up again. Then, after her father kisses her goodnight, they both fall into a restless sleep.

Angel wakes to a loud crash. She sits bolt upright on her banig and realises the mat is soaking wet. Teeming rain is pouring into the roof-space where a sheet of iron has just been torn off by the wind. *So much for the roof looking good*, she thinks. The roar of the storm is deafeningly close and the whole house is shaking as if it's about to be flung into the sky just like she was flung off the boat in her nightmare.

She wishes she could go back to sleep rather than face the frightening reality of the typhoon, but there's no sleeping in this racket. She stretches as best she can in the cramped roof cavity and yawns hard with a shiver.

'Papa,' she calls out, but her voice is drowned beneath the din. 'Papa!' she shouts louder. No answer.

The wind is building in strength and Angel is sure it will continue to get worse. Even as it whistles around the little house, making the hairs stand up on her arms, she can sense it has not yet reached its full power.

She climbs down the ladder into the living area, feeling her way to the ledge for the candles and matches that she tucked away the other day. Although it's almost morning the house is dark. Even with a candle lit, the room remains a mass of sinister shadows.

'Papa?'

She can see now that the table has been pushed away and her father is gone. She dares not open the door, but she peers through a narrow crack in the little window covered with the heavy cardboard. There's nothing to see, just a wall of silvery grey water pouring from the black sky.

'Papa?'

Someone is moving outside near the taklub post where the boat has been dragged clear of the angry waves. It must be her father making sure the little bangka is tied fast against the surge of the sea.

There's nothing Angel can do about the hole in the roof. She only hopes that the rest of it stays on. She crouches in a corner that is still relatively dry and burrows in. *Perhaps if I'm very small,* she thinks, *the storm won't see me.* She wonders about Mrs Reyes next door, hoping her house is still in one piece.

Angel stays in this position for a while, shifting uncomfortably on the concrete floor, waiting for her father to come back. She has no idea what time it is, but every second feels like a minute and every minute an hour.

She thinks about her mother and brothers, wishes that she could be sure they made it safely to her grandparents' house. She picks up the old mobile phone but the signal is dead already. Along with the power, the storm has knocked out the phone system. Even so, she uselessly presses buttons, willing it to suddenly wake up, then sighs and switches it off to save the battery. Hopefully the phone and power will come back on tomorrow, once the storm has passed. *This isn't so bad,* she thinks, *just a lot of rain and wind and a loose bit of roof.*

At that moment there's an unearthly shriek as the wind increases another few notches. Angel can barely hear herself think. The door flies open and her father staggers in, drenched, bending his whole weight against it to push it closed. Angel jumps up to help and when the door's finally shut they pull the table and chairs back across to brace it.

'It's almost upon us,' her father shouts close to her ear. He hugs her tightly. Angel's been doing pretty well up until now, but she's suddenly very frightened and she clings to her father.

Her mind fills with terrifying images; she sees the storm collecting all of the houses and cars and trucks and jeepneys in Tacloban and throwing them into a giant blender where they're crashing and smashing into each other, a whirling mass of wood and metal.

The roof of the house creaks with strain as the fingers of the storm reach in under the eaves, each gust weakening the nuts and bolts and nails that hold it in place. Even over the roar of the wind she can hear awful noises outside, things falling and blowing and belting into each other. A few times she hears a human shout or scream, so high pitched with fear that it cuts through to where she and her father are sheltering. 'Please keep us safe, Lord,' she repeats to herself over and over, praying that their house, built with so much love and care, will stand up to Yolanda's attack.

There's a crunch and a crash as something collapses outside. The house rattles as a heavy object hits the other side of the wall. Another sheet peels off the roof with a tearing shriek, opening them up to the wind and the incessant rain.

Angel can hear another sound now, too. A deep shuddering roar. It's the sea.

She and her brothers have grown up fishing and swimming and playing in the sea. It's a central part of their lives and they have come to understand its moods. But today it's unknowable – raging and unpredictable. She remembers hearing that during a typhoon it's not only the wind that causes death and destruction, but also the sea, which rises up and swallows the shore. She is gripped by a sudden moment of clarity.

'Papa, we have to climb up.' She shakes Juan from where he's peering out through the little crack at the window. 'We need to move, the ocean is coming,' she yells.

'You're right, quick, up the ladder, go!' he shouts. Angel scrambles for the bamboo rungs. Her father reaches for the phone and a small canvas bag of valuables that he hoists over his head and clasps securely across his body.

'Hurry, Papa, hurry,' Angel cries back at him. She's unable to see him clearly in the gloom below her, and longs to feel his steadying hand letting her know he is close behind.

There's an ear-splitting crash as the first wave jumps the shoreline and engulfs everything in its path. Angel has barely made it to the roof-space before the sea hurls itself at the little house, forcing open the door and gushing through the window.

Angel screams, feeling it grab at her ankles. The ladder is torn away just as she jumps onto the roof beam, but she's still not high enough. Water is up to her chin and she and Juan are fighting to keep their heads above its churning mass. And then it's in her nose and in her mouth and she's gasping in panic and swallowing more. The house is completely swamped. There's no space left to breathe and her head keeps hitting the ceiling. She's stuck under the salty sea in her own bedroom. It's pitch dark and there's no escape.

Angel almost gives up.

Somehow, she thinks she can see her father's dark shape in the water.

'Angel,' he's shouting. 'Angel, swim up, SWIM UP!'

She tries but she's so tired now. It's too hard.

Angel begins to feel herself drifting away and down... but then something pushes her up hard from below. A hand is clasping her wrist from above, and then another hand grabs her by the shoulder, hauling her up and out through the hole in the roof where the sheet was torn off earlier.

'Papa?'

It's Mrs Reyes. 'Breathe, child,' the woman cries. 'Hold on tightly, and breathe.'

Angel gasps and breathes and vomits and gasps. She can't get enough air; her throat feels clogged with salt and spew. The storm is still tearing at her, trying to fling her off the roof, or to sweep her away into the surging sea. Mrs Reyes has an iron grip though. She clings to Angel with one arm and the roof with the other. But another wave is coming and this one is bigger and stronger. It pushes them so high and with such viciousness that they can no longer hold on to the roof. They let go and the house disappears below them. The young girl and the old woman cling to each other as they're sucked into the raging torrent.

It's so very dark. The wind is howling like a beast. The rain stabs like pins into their upturned faces as they're swirled around like rag dolls. 'Papa! Papa!' Angel is desperate for any sign of her father as the water sweeps her away, but he's vanished.

In the gloom cars fly past; razor-sharp sheets of metal, planks of wood, fuel drums, whole boats, pieces of furniture are all now flotsam. Angel and Mrs Reyes are just two of many people fighting for their lives, desperately trying to find a stable foothold or something to hang on to that's not moving.

Eventually Angel is snagged across the chest by a long, thick cable. It winds her at first but she grabs it. It's a little loose, and she and Mrs Reyes, still clinging to each other, are pulled up short as the current propels them forward. Angel's shoulder is stretched to breaking point but she resists the urge to let go. With a chill she realises that she's holding on to what should be a deadly powerline, but there's no electricity running through it now. The water must be very deep. In Tacloban the powerlines are more than two storeys high.

Hand over hand, Angel drags herself along the line and Mrs Reyes follows behind. The water continues to tug at them, but at last they reach the power pole that the wire is attached to. Angel climbs onto a cross bar and hauls Mrs Reyes up next to her. They climb up as high as they can, one either side of the T-bar, and wrap themselves around it like caterpillars on a twig. Then they hold on grimly as the water rages beneath them and the wind does its best to topple them off.

With their heads so close together, Angel can see now that Mrs Reyes is in a bad way. Her eyes are clenched shut and her face is tight with pain. She shouts right in the old woman's ear.

'Mrs Reyes, stay with me. Don't let go.'

'I'm trying, anak ko, little one. I'm just so tired…'

'You saved me!'

Mrs Reyes lifts her head and looks into Angel's eyes. 'It was God's will.'

'How? How did you know I was in the roof?'

'The waves were coming. I climbed. Water lifted me and dropped me on your roof. I saw you. I saw your hand reaching. I grabbed it.'

'You saved me, Mrs Reyes. You saved my life.'

'It was a miracle, child. God wants you to live.'

'Papa. Did you see him?'

Mrs Reyes closes her eyes again and rests her head on the power pole. She needs all her strength just to keep holding on.

A gust of wind slams into them and with only one hand clinging on, Angel suddenly loses her balance and her body flips to the underside of the T-bar. Now she's swinging by an arm and a leg and all she can see is the churning black sea below, reaching up to engulf and swallow her…

Six

Somehow, Angel manages to swing her dangling arm back over the pole and then slowly – finger by finger – she pulls herself up and hitches her body on top of the T-bar again. Gaping at her in horror, Mrs Reyes shimmies forward and clasps her forearms over the top of Angel's, binding them together for added strength.

The old woman shouts over the wind: 'Hold fast. No letting go – you hear me? We are going to make it, you and I. We will get through this together.'

And this is how they remain for the next few hours. Clinging to the power pole like monkeys. They're lucky it stands up to the wind and the water. As it begins to get light the rain is so heavy they still can't see much. But they can hear buildings creaking and tearing, disintegrating all around them. The crunching and collapsing combined with the noise of the storm is deafening.

When it finally stops, Angel's ears are ringing. Her head aches and her skin stings. Every muscle screams from holding the same position at the top of the pole for so long, and she feels as though her fingers will never unbend, they've been gripping so tightly.

'It's over,' Mrs Reyes finally says, in a shaky whisper. 'Come now, the danger has passed.'

When Angel lifts her head she registers there's barely a breeze. The sky is still grey, but it's pale now, not dark like before. From her high vantage point she can see the sea, still choppy, in the distance. Carefully, she raises her body and, straddling the T-bar, she looks around her.

Her city is unrecognisable. It has been destroyed. In its place are mountains of jagged timber, great chunks of broken cement, smashed furniture and piles of jeepneys. There are cars and motorbikes hanging from trees. Even more bizarre, in the middle of it all is a huge fishing boat, at least twenty-five metres long, perched precariously on top of a pile of rubble. Everywhere is brown and grey and black. The rich green tropical vegetation has been wiped out.

'Oh, Yolanda,' she breathes in awe. 'What have you done?'

Tears are streaming down Mrs Reyes' face. 'There's nothing left,' she murmurs. 'Tacloban is lost.'

Far into the distance Angel can see the dome of the convention centre. She can also just make out Santo Niño Church. They both look okay, but there's barely a single building left in between. She tries to work out where her own house should be but it's impossible to detect shapes beneath the ocean of debris and churned-up water that's covering every square centimetre of space. Somehow she will have to find her home in this mess. And she will have to find her father.

Her hand jerks to her throat. Incredibly, the pearl is still there on its golden chain, tucked beneath the collar of her shredded polo shirt. Its smooth, silky surface comforts her and reminds her of her father's words: *I am with you.* A small comfort, at least.

Towards the foreshore Angel can see people already climbing around on piles of splintered wood and smashed cement that used to be houses. She resolves to head towards them first.

She turns again to Mrs Reyes, who is watching her with pity in her eyes.

'You must prepare yourself for the worst, child,' the woman says softly.

Angel wriggles along the cross beam to the central post. Although they are high above the road, there's so much debris piled up that all she has to do is slide down the power pole a short distance and step down onto it. Mrs Reyes does the same, Angel holding her arms out to catch the older woman.

Both of them look appalling. They're covered in cuts and bruises. Mrs Reyes has a black eye and there's a nasty slash on her face that is open and weeping. Angel is covered in bleeding scratches and her hair is one giant knot. Their clothes are filthy and torn and both have lost their shoes, which is immediately a problem as they begin to pick their way through the splintered wood and sheets of buckled tin and shattered cement. Angel cries out as she treads on a nail sticking out of a piece of timber. She inches her foot off the sharp, rusty spike and watches the blood ooze from the wound. Mrs Reyes is concerned. 'You'll need a shot for that,' she says. But where will they find a doctor in this chaos? They turn and look across the tangled landscape bathed in dull, glassy light.

A woman is squatting beside a hut that has been flattened by a concrete wall, weeping inconsolably. Further on a man is frantically digging around the edges of a collapsed building, a little girl sitting nearby watching him with empty eyes. Sights like these make Angel's heart ache, but she is as helpless as they are. All she can do is continue to make her way over slabs of roof, along broken timber beams and unstable, teetering pieces of cement. Occasionally there's a thick black powerline snaking through the debris. Angel and Mrs Reyes avoid them carefully. The electricity appears to be off, but it's hard to know for sure if every line is dead.

More survivors are beginning to crawl out from underneath buildings or down from high spots where they escaped from the surge. Dozens emerge from a school building that sits in an elevated position, undamaged apart from a partially torn off roof.

Everyone moves slowly, dazed and traumatised. Angel asks people if they have seen her father and they look at her with blank expressions. Some speak to the desperate young girl with sympathy, but most of them are in their own quiet hell, searching for loved ones, just like her. Here and there lie what look like bundles of clothes, but when Angel steps over one she sees a tangle of dark hair and a leg twisted at an impossible angle. She lets out a whimper. It's the body of a young man. She doesn't recognise the partly obscured face but she knows that it could easily be one of her schoolmates. Mrs Reyes comes up beside her and says, 'Poor soul.' The old lady leans forward and covers his face with a piece of tin. 'Someone will take care of him. He's at peace now.'

From then on, Angel avoids anything that looks like it might be a body. All around people are collecting the dead. Some are howling in grief; others just stare in shock. It seems like every single survivor is searching for someone, expecting the worst.

Angel is worried about her father, very worried, but she refuses to believe that he is dead. Juan is a tough and resourceful man. She has to believe that he is safe and it gives her the strength to keep going.

Slowly the young girl and the old woman pick their way over and through the mounds of debris. They are heading in the direction of home, although with no landmarks it's difficult to work out exactly where that is. Angel is amazed that they were swept so far by the surging water; a kilometre or two at least.

She thinks she knows where the house might be but each time she scales a mountain there's another ahead of her and her bearings shift again. She scans the mess for a glimpse of the faded green of Mrs Reyes's house or the taklub post on the shoreline in front of hers, but there's no sign of either. The reality is that her father's house may be among the many dwellings now lying in pieces under her feet.

Their progress becomes painfully slow. Mrs Reyes is starting to wheeze as the dreadful ordeal finally catches up with her. Every so often she lets out a gasp and points at another bizarre sight: a boat hundreds of metres from the shoreline or a couch hanging from a tree or a TV dangling from a power pole.

Angel limps on ahead and is first to reach the shoreline, where her feet sink into the ankle-deep mud and sludge. There's a small boat lying upside down and with a start, Angel realises it's her father's bangka. It appears to be relatively undamaged. No doubt the engine is past saving and turning the boat back over will need the strength of a few men, but it's a sign that they must be close to home.

Her mind fills with the memory of her father outside securing the boat amid the screaming wind and rain. She was sure he was going to be blown away. Then the moment when he pushed her up and out of the water into the arms of Mrs Reyes. Angel has no doubt it was he who instigated her miracle rescue and tears threaten to burst through again. How she longs for her home, but at the same time she is terrified of what she might find there.

Scanning the mounds of rubble further along the shore, her eye catches on something familiar. It's the Filipino flag from Mrs Reyes's flagpole lying in the mud. Beyond it, bits of splintered green timber create a trail of sorts that she follows until it stops. She looks up at a pile of broken planks. They are propping up some sheets of tin that lean like an awning across the front of her family's house. It's still standing!

Angel is flooded with a bittersweet relief. Her knees go weak and she sinks down into the mud. She wonders how she is going to get inside when the door is totally buried under debris. Mrs Reyes limps up to her and hands her a bottle of water and a bag of potato chips. Angel realises that it's some time since she had anything to eat or drink.

'I took them from the ruins of the store,' the old woman explains, looking a little guilty. 'We have to eat.' She holds up a plastic shopping bag with a few bottles of water and some soggy snacks. 'It's not much, but it should get us through today.' She lowers herself onto the wet ground next to Angel. They open a bottle each and drink deeply and then share the packet of potato chips and a mushy chocolate bar between them.

Eventually Mrs Reyes takes a deep breath and heaves herself up. Step by step she makes her way over to the spot where her house once stood. There's nothing left but a cement slab blanketed in debris. The old woman shuffles around, shaking her head and muttering as she picks up the odd small item. She starts making a pile: a muddy tea towel, a metal spoon, a saucepan, the shards of a china plate and a couple of smeared family photographs, which she wipes on her torn clothes before placing them carefully on top.

Angel gets up and walks back to the flag that she spied half-buried in the sludge. She picks it up and rinses it in a muddy puddle as best she can and places it next to the meagre pile of possessions. Angel contemplates all that remains of the kind old woman's long, busy life and drops her head into her hands, overwhelmed. Mrs Reyes stops her fossicking and puts her arm around the child.

'Don't worry for me, dear, I don't need much, and houses can be rebuilt.'

It's true.

Angel regards her own broken home, still standing but now without roof or windows. She is sure her father could fix it; he's so clever at repairing things.

In the meantime she has to assess the damage. It's her job to look after their home now. She pulls half-heartedly at a sheet of tin that's covering the door but she knows she can't go in that way; it's too dangerous. She steps back for a moment and considers her options.

'I'm going to have to climb in,' she says, thinking aloud.

Mrs Reyes agrees. 'Yes, I think that's the only way. Careful of sharp bits!'

Angel begins a slow crawl up the pile of rubble leaning against the wall, doing her best to avoid nails and splinters and slicing edges of tin. It's not easy, especially without shoes. By the time she reaches the top of the wall and pauses on the small remaining corner of roof her hands are dotted with tiny splinters of wood and she has another deep cut on her foot. She looks over the expanse of wreckage for a moment. The sea is almost calm, but littered with junk floating on the surface. She looks towards Samar where her mother and brothers should be. The sun is high in the sky now and as often happens after typhoons, there are already patches of blue. It will rain again later, but for the moment Yolanda's shocking aftermath is fully illuminated.

Angel swings her legs over the roof and peers down into her home. The table and chairs are tipped upside down; pots and pans and utensils have been torn from their hooks and litter the room; bedding is strewn around, wet and muddy. There's spilt rice and broken jars and plates all over the place. Black sludge smears the walls and lies deep on the cement floor. Her brothers' twin teddy bears that they've had since they were babies lie face down in the mud.

All the careful packing away of their household items was a wasted effort. Hanging the kitchen utensils on nails, folding the bedding and clothes and stacking them into the roof, boxing up food and placing it high out of harm's way – undone in an instant.

Angel half-slides, half-climbs off the roof into what remains of the living room. She lands in a puddle of mud and water, wincing from the pain in her cut feet. Slowly she wades around, inspecting the damage. There's nothing much that's salvageable apart from perhaps some cutlery and some pots and pans. She picks up the old mobile phone and tosses it back into the mud again. Useless. She spends a few minutes making a pile of some things that she might wash and try to save. Eventually she turns over a chair and sits down.

She looks up through the roof at the sky, dark clouds slowly passing over and the occasional flash of blue. The smell of salted fish is gone; now the house reeks of mud and salt water.

Jammed in the corner is a wet bag of clothes upended in the mud. She pulls out a T-shirt and a pair of old cut-off jeans and changes into them. They're damp, but anything is better than the ripped and shredded clothes she's been wearing. At the bottom of the bag is a pair of damp canvas shoes and she jams them onto her filthy, blood-smeared feet. A pair of her mother's old sandals, buckled together, are floating in the mud. They will work for Mrs Reyes. There's nothing more to do here. Grimly she climbs up, swings her legs over the wall and descends the rubble.

Mrs Reyes is sitting on the seawall and she looks up as Angel approaches, but says nothing.

Angel shakes her head. She puts the sandals down and sits next to Mrs Reyes.

She's found her home but what of her mother and her brothers? She has no way of knowing whether the storm hit Samar with the same ferocity as this. *Are they alive? Where is Papa? Where is my family?*

Angel and Mrs Reyes sit on the seawall for a long time, too exhausted to make any plans. When dark starts to descend, Angel collects some dirty but relatively dry blankets and the two of them crawl into the narrow space made by the sheets of tin propped against the wall of Angel's house. As soon as they lie down they fall into a deep sleep.

Seven

When she wakes at dawn, Angel knows what she has to do.

'Everyone will be at the church. It's still standing and it's safe. That's where I'll find my father.'

Mrs Reyes still looks exhausted, but she nods wearily. After dipping their faces and hands in a bucket of cloudy rainwater, they set off in the direction of Santo Niño.

The journey is slow and difficult because there's so much mess obstructing their progress, and Angel soon realises she is desperately hungry. She and Mrs Reyes have had nothing to eat since yesterday when they finished the snacks collected from the wrecked store. There's not so much to scavenge now. Too many people have had the same idea and what's left is wet and spoiling.

They're thirsty, too. Water is an even bigger problem than food. The taps are not working and the water in the creeks and ponds is too dirty to drink. Angel observes some desperate people scooping water out of a puddle and filling buckets but she knows that the water will make them sick. It's full of debris from the storm and brackish from the salty sea.

She runs her tongue around the inside of her dry mouth. They have to get a drink soon. They've been walking for several hours and Mrs Reyes is flagging. Angel can't remember it being this far to the church.

The two of them sit quietly on top of a pile of smashed-up timber. All around below them people are at work, pulling out salvageable items, retrieving things like mangled bicycles and motos, building makeshift shelters from pieces of wood and sheets of iron. Many are using bricks and chunks of wood as hammers; others have managed to salvage the odd useful tool from the mess. A few families have commandeered a large boat that's teetering atop the rubble. They are sleeping in its cargo hold, which stinks of fish, but at least it's out of the rain. There are still fairly constant heavy showers interspersed with the occasional burst of hot, steamy sunshine and the sickly smell of death and decay is pervasive in the afternoon heat.

'Shall we get going again?' Angel asks Mrs Reyes gently.

The old woman has her eyes closed, resting. For a moment Angel thinks she must be asleep but then she nods wearily. 'Yes, my dear. We must push on.'

Angel helps her to her feet. 'You know, I do wonder why the government isn't handing out water and food yet. Where's the army?' Mrs Reyes says.

Angel nods in agreement. Water, power and phones are all still down. It's more than a full day after the storm and they've seen no sign of any help. She squints into the distance. The church is still a long way off.

'Let's find somewhere to sleep before it gets dark. We'll make better progress tomorrow after we've had some rest.'

The two of them hobble along. Angel's cuts and bruises are aching now. She's concerned about the wound on Mrs Reyes's face. It's weeping red fluid and very angry looking. As well as food and water, they really need a doctor. Angel feels completely helpless and more than a little scared.

I don't know what to do, she repeats over and over in her head. *I don't know what to do. I wish Papa was here.* She struggles to hold back tears as they trudge along through the wreckage. Everything is so bleak. The smell of rot is everywhere. People are pressing pieces of cloth to their mouths and noses, but it's impossible to completely block it out.

They are near the centre of what used to be the city and everyone looks exhausted and desperate. So far, Angel has not seen a single person that she recognises. *They all evacuated before the storm hit, or they're safe at the church*, she tells herself. But she only half believes it.

She slows down to wait for Mrs Reyes, who is trailing along behind, progressing at a snail's pace now. She helps the old woman climb over a mountain of rice that has spilled out of a storage warehouse. The water from the storm has washed tons of it out into the street and it's wet and stinking as it ferments in the sunshine. The rice squelches under her feet. It's absolutely disgusting. She holds her breath, trying to block her nose, but it's unavoidable. The sour stench will stay with her for days, in her hair, on her clothes, the taste of it stuck in her throat. She gags uncontrollably as she and Mrs Reyes slide down the other side of the sludgy pile. She can't understand why people are collecting the rice in buckets and tubs and then she's aghast when she realises why. 'They're not going to eat that, surely?'

The old woman nods. 'People are hungry, child.' She looks grey and exhausted. She puts her hand on her chest, breathing heavily.

'I'm not sure that I can go much further,' she tells Angel. 'My heart is fluttering.'

Angel looks around worriedly. They need somewhere dry and safe where Mrs Reyes can rest, and she must find them some water at least. She scans the surroundings for any landmark that she might recognise, trying to get her bearings. At first it all looks the same, just piles and piles of broken and damaged buildings, but her gaze settles on a hand-painted sign.

'WE NEED FOOD!' it says. 'BARANGAY 18.'

'That's where Issy lives!' she exclaims. She knows the way to Issy's house well.

'Come,' she says excitedly to Mrs Reyes. 'This way!'

They start down the narrow alley. It's full of mud and junk, but a few houses have survived Yolanda's fury. Angel is quaking inside as she shepherds Mrs Reyes through the debris. What has happened to her friend?

She thinks of the last time she saw Issy, that afternoon at school when her mother and brothers came to fetch her. Before the storm, before everything changed.

Angel wonders how long it will be before they can go to school again. She wonders if the school is even still there. She sends a quick and silent prayer for her teacher, Mrs Fernandez, and the other students. Absently her hand goes to her neck where the pearl hangs safely on its chain, tucked beneath her T-shirt. She squeezes it tightly, sending another wish to the heavens, for her father.

Mrs Reyes is barely able to walk when they reach a rickety gate, hanging by one hinge and propped open with a piece of broken cement. Someone has placed some long planks through the gateway and into the house, forming a kind of bridge across a sea of mud. Much has changed, but Angel is sure that this is Issy's house and she calls out: 'Issy! Issy! Are you here? Oh, please be here…'

A figure with a sweep of dark hair is crouched over a small cooking fire on the porch. She looks up and jumps to her feet when she sees who it is.

'Angel!' Issy exclaims. 'Thank God you are safe!' For a moment, Angel doesn't recognise her friend with her drab clothes and unkempt hair, but her warm smile is unmistakeable.

The two girls run to each other and hug tightly.

'You made it!' Angel cries joyfully.

'We all did, but only just…' says Issy.

Angel turns to Mrs Reyes, who is leaning against the gate.

'Mrs Reyes and I made it through the storm together. She saved me.'

Issy nods seriously. 'I am so glad to see you again, Mrs Reyes.'

'She's not well,' says Angel. 'Can we rest here for the night?'

'Of course,' says Issy with concern and the two girls support Mrs Reyes on either side as they move her into the house.

When Issy's mother sees Angel, she pulls her into a fierce embrace. Normally very careful with her appearance, Maria is wearing a stained shirt and trousers and her hair is covered in a scarf.

'Veronica will be beside herself with worry. I wish we could tell her you are safe, but there is no communication anywhere in the city.'

'So the whole network is down?' asks Angel.

'Yes, but even if it was up all the phone batteries are flat. With no electricity there's no way to charge them.'

Angel explains everything that happened to her as the three of them prepare some food amid the wreckage of the living space. Issy's house is more substantial than Angel's, reflecting her father's higher income. The walls are cement brick and there are three separate rooms, a small fridge and even a television. Today the house is still standing and the roof is still on, but the water has damaged everything inside. The electrical goods are ruined, the furniture is broken and all the other household items are damp and filthy.

The family and their surviving neighbours have

collected whatever provisions they can find from the nearby store and Issy's father and brother are out looking for more. They have flour and some tinned sardines, and a small amount of bottled water that Issy and Maria readily share. Angel and Mrs Reyes struggle not to gulp it down, they're so thirsty.

Issy and Angel prepare some flat cakes with the flour and fry them in a pan over the fire. It's not much, but Angel still can't help gobbling her share down. Mrs Reyes only manages a little. The old woman falls asleep on a damp mat on the cement floor under the watchful eye of Maria.

'She needs a doctor,' she whispers to Angel.

They observe Mrs Reyes's chest as it rises and falls erratically in her sleep.

'I will go tomorrow into the centre and find what help there is,' Angel vows.

She also needs treatment for her cuts, especially the one on her foot, which is becoming infected from walking around in the putrid slush. Issy's mother does her best to wash it but she has very little clean water and no antiseptic. There's only so much she can do.

Just before nightfall, Issy's father, Danilo, trudges through the door, carrying a plastic bag.

'It's not much, but…' He spots Mrs Reyes first and frowns in confusion at the old lady asleep in the middle of the floor. Then he looks up and sees Angel.

'Thank goodness.' He hugs her with genuine relief. Seeing him reminds Angel of her own father. Danilo is chubby and bald, always cheerful, where Juan is slim and wiry with a serious demeanour, but they are both loving fathers who are devoted to their families.

'How are the others?' he asks hesitantly.

Angel doesn't trust herself to speak so she shrugs helplessly, her eyes shiny with tears.

Justin comes in then, looking even wearier than his father. His cargo pants are shredded and his long fringe is dirty and matted with salt as he pushes it out of his eyes. When he sees his sister's friend the grim line of his mouth lifts just a little.

'Good to see you, pipsqueak,' he says solemnly.

Eight

After dark, the two girls go outside and sit on the porch. Issy has found a comb and she gently begins to tease out her friend's knotted hair. As she works, Issy explains how she and her family survived.

'The water flowed into the house up to the roof, so we swam out and climbed up that pole there.'

She points to a sturdy post that forms the corner of the front fence with a broken streetlight still attached to the top.

'All of us climbed up and just clung on there with the water washing around us. It went on for hours. How we all held on to a single pole for so long, I don't know. We were one above the other, holding on to each other's legs. It was so exhausting and scary.'

Issy shakes her head, remembering the long, long night and morning.

Angel tells her friend how she was separated from Juan and how the flood dragged her and Mrs Reyes through the wreckage until they latched on to the electricity cable.

'You were so lucky the power was off!' Issy gasps.

The two teenagers sit silently together in the dark. Angel's hair is smooth and knot-free now, and Issy plaits it into a single neat rope.

'We're all lucky, you know,' says Issy quietly. 'So many people have died here. The family next door all drowned, hugging each other.'

'Yes, you're right,' Angel agrees. She takes the comb and slides it through her friend's shoulder-length tresses with sure, comforting strokes. She knows that she's lucky to be alive but she can't feel any real sense of relief or happiness until she finds her parents and brothers. 'Why is the government not helping us?' she complains. 'Why are the phones still not working?'

Issy can only shrug.

'I've heard a few planes flying over but I haven't seen any sign of help yet,' she says.

The barangay is inky black with no electricity. Only small pinpricks of light from cooking fires and candles glimmer in the dark. Issy and Angel doze on the front porch, where it's cooler than inside the house, although mosquitoes whine incessantly. Around midnight the girls are suddenly snapped awake by loud voices down the lane. It sounds like a group of men arguing. Then there's a loud bang.

Danilo bursts through the front door.

'Girls, inside quickly,' he urges them.

'What is it?' Angel asks sleepily. The two girls

scramble inside the house as the yelling gets louder and the shots get closer.

Maria and Justin are wide awake.

'Is that gunshots?' Mrs Reyes is concerned but disoriented and weak, reluctant to move from her mat on the floor.

'Looters,' Danilo answers grimly. 'As if things aren't bad enough already, now they want to steal the little we have. Quickly, we need to hide some of the food.'

Issy and her mother gather the tinned fish, a bag each of flour and rice and a bottle of oil and hide it all under a pile of damp bedrolls along with the last of the bottled water. They're only just in time. A group of men burst through the gate, shouting and waving pistols. A couple have bigger guns, long rifles like the ones that soldiers from the Filipino military carry. Angel counts six men, ragged and dirty, with torn pieces of cloth tied around their faces to conceal their identities.

'Food! All of it!' demands the one at the front, who seems to be the leader. Two of the others are carrying crude torches and they wave the naked flames dangerously around the room, searching for anything to take.

'We don't have much,' Danilo says calmly. 'You are welcome to share it.'

'We will not share, we will take all that you have,' sneers the leader.

Cowering in the corner with Angel and Maria, Issy starts to whimper in fear. One of the thugs stops searching and looks them over. He reaches out and touches Angel on the cheek and she slaps him away. Before the man can react Mrs Reyes hisses loudly, 'Get away from her. Beast!' The old woman wobbles to her feet and steadies herself on a broken chair. Next to her, Justin glares threateningly, his arms crossed tightly in front of him. The man looks at them for a moment, then lets out a cackle and resumes the hunt for food.

Danilo remains steady. 'We will show you what we have,' he says, nudging Maria towards the supplies that they deliberately didn't hide: some bags of flour, rice and a few blackened bananas that he and Justin scavenged that day. The looters snatch up the items, shoving Issy and Angel in the process. The girls do not react.

'Thanks for your kind hospitality,' the leader sniggers as he heads towards the door.

Mrs Reyes glares at the tall, muscular man with a pistol in one hand and a sack of rice in the other.

'Shame on you,' she says defiantly. 'There is no courage in stealing food from children and the destitute.'

For a moment he looks uncertain, shifting uncomfortably from foot to foot.

He opens his mouth to protest but she raises a hand.

'Go now,' she commands him. 'Don't even think of coming back!'

To everyone's relief, the looters turn and leave. As soon as they have gone, Justin turns on Angel.

'Well, that was stupid, hitting that creep. You could have set them all off.'

'You would have done exactly the same thing,' Angel says angrily.

'No, I would have thought about it first...'

'Enough!' orders Maria. 'It's over. Now get some sleep!'

But even after they calm down and all is quiet again, Angel is wakeful, startling at every tiny noise. When the dawn finally comes she feels relieved, and thoroughly drained.

In the grey light she shifts uncomfortably on her mat on the porch, watching Danilo, who is repairing and reinforcing the gate. She shudders when she considers how horribly wrong last night could have gone. Survivors had been talking about armed men looting since the storm but she didn't really believe it could be true. Now she knows it is. It's one thing to take a few things to feed yourself in a crisis, as most have done, but violent, organised looting is another thing altogether.

Angel is more determined than ever to find her father and get help. Today she will push on to the church, leaving Mrs Reyes who is far too unwell to go further. She has barely stirred from her place on the floor where she collapsed as soon as the looters departed. Her lined face is bathed in sweat and her breathing is fast and shallow.

A distant, somehow familiar sound interrupts Angel's thoughts. Danilo hears it too. He stops what he's doing and goes out into the street. Angel follows and the two of them stand together, eyes scanning the sky, listening intently. Seconds later, a helicopter appears above them, hovering like a dragonfly. The Filipino flag is clearly emblazoned on the side of the aircraft and Danilo bellows: 'AT LAST!'

The military has arrived.

The helicopter hovers briefly overhead and then swoops over and past them, low and smooth.

'Quickly, it's landing,' Danilo shouts. 'They might have supplies. Hurry!'

The two of them set off in the direction of the chopper, with Issy and Justin close behind. They run along the narrow lane, dodging all the clutter, and out onto the main road. There's a large expanse of open land a few streets away and Danilo leads them towards it. Sure enough, as they round the corner they see not one but two large military choppers hovering a few metres above the ground, surrounded by a quickly expanding crowd.

'Hurry, kids, hurry,' Danilo huffs.

Around the aircraft it's chaos as people jostle for bags of rice and packs of bottled water. The helicopter blades are whipping up mud and leaves and sticks, adding to the frantic atmosphere as the sound of the engines blends with the shouting on the ground. It's clear there won't be enough for everyone. Soldiers throw bags of rice one or two at a time out the open doors of the choppers along with the water packs. Frantic people pounce and wrestle each other for the spoils. Angel and the others stand back and watch, reluctant to get caught up in the mayhem.

Those who manage to grab a bag of rice or some water heave it onto their shoulders and hurry away as fast as they can. Gradually the crowd disperses as supplies dwindle until one last bag of rice is dumped out the door. Then the choppers begin to rise into the air.

Empty handed, Angel watches the soldiers hanging out the doorways, legs dangling. One catches her eye as his craft starts to pulls away. He gives her a nod and a half salute, then shouts something to her, pointing towards the centre of Tacloban. She strains to hear but the chopper is too noisy. Then they're gone.

The four of them watch the helicopters head towards Tacloban Airport until they are just dark specks in the sky.

'What do you think that guy was saying?' Angel asks Issy.

'I'm not sure, but he was pointing towards the city centre. Perhaps there are more supplies there?'

'Do you think they'll come back?' Issy asks her father, who is deep in discussion with some of the other bystanders.

'Apparently, there's a big staging point being set up at the airport,' says Danilo. 'Food and water is being brought in as well as medical supplies. They are also going to start evacuating people who want to go to Manila.'

'Will we go, Dad?' Issy asks. The family has many relatives in the capital.

'I think it's better to stay here once we have enough food and water. This is our home and we will protect it and repair it,' he says. 'Those planes should be for those more needy than us: the old, the sick and the orphaned.'

His gaze rests on Angel for only a split second but she catches it. *He thinks my parents are dead*, she realises with a dull ache. She knows that it may be true. Perhaps she is an orphan now. She shakes the thought away.

She wonders about Mrs Reyes, who is elderly and unwell. Her home is gone. Perhaps she would prefer to go to Manila to be with her sons?

'The UN has arrived too,' Danilo explains. 'There's help coming from countries all over the region. America and Australia are also sending supplies and doctors.'

Right on cue there's a deep rumbling sound. Angel scans the horizon.

'There!' announces Issy, pointing. It's a huge, fat-bellied cargo plane, coming in low and steady.

Angel squints at the flag on the aircraft's tail. *What's in it and where did it come from?* she wonders. *Who is coming to help us?*

The plane passes over them with a deafening roar.

'Royal Australian Air Force', she spells out along its side. It's so low she can even see a picture of a red kangaroo. The moment it's gone, there's another dull drone in the distance and another speck on the horizon. They count six enormous military planes that morning: two from the Philippine Air Force, and one each from Australia, Singapore, Thailand and the USA.

Finally, help is here.

When they get back to the house, Angel is eager to get going, but Maria doesn't want her to make the journey alone to the church.

'The planes have only just arrived and today they are unloading. Tomorrow they will be set up and ready to help you.'

'What about Papa?'

'How will you find him in all the chaos? Believe me, Angel, it's better to wait for twenty-four hours.'

Maria cups her hands gently around the girl's face. 'There are bad people out there. You saw those men last night. They think they can do what they like. Your mother would never forgive me for letting you go while Tacloban is still in this lawless state.'

She is right about Veronica, and Angel knows it. Reluctantly she agrees to wait until tomorrow.

That afternoon, after they have scavenged some packets of dried noodles and tins of beef loaf, she and Issy walk down to the waterfront, where the sea is full of sticks and plastic and vehicles and upturned boats. A small clean-up crew is at work using big poles and nets to pull junk out of the water. Here and there in the shallows people are collecting bits and pieces and piling everything up in orderly pyramids along the shoreline.

The girls pitch in to help, collecting small unsalvageable things and dumping them on the rubbish heaps. There are lots of broken household items, sodden pillows and cushions and pieces of clothing. Angel picks up a small dirty-grey teddy bear that once would have been blue. Around its neck is a frayed ribbon with a bell on it. She remembers with a jolt the muddy bears at home and feels a rush of worry about Cristian and Carlo. She wonders where the child who took it to bed every night is now and she stuffs it into her pocket. It doesn't seem right to throw away someone's precious toy.

Nine

After a restless night, Angel wakes early and prepares to set out for the church. Justin and Danilo have already gone out to find more materials to barricade the door against intruders. They were all badly shaken by the ease with which the looters had gained entry. Maria seems even more reluctant to let her go.

'In broad daylight I'll be fine,' reasons Angel. 'It's still early and there are plenty of people about. I will get to Santo Niño in a few hours.'

'Let Justin go with you; he'll be back soon, I'm sure,' pleads the woman.

'He's needed here,' protests Angel. 'Your family needs to find food and water and secure the house.'

There's no arguing with that.

'I promise I won't take any chances. And when I get to the church I will find my father and we will be back with medicine and food before it gets dark.'

The truth is, Angel would prefer to have someone go with her, but there is so much to be done here, they need all hands on deck, especially with more mouths to feed.

Angel says goodbye to Issy and Maria and hugs Mrs Reyes. The old lady is propped up on the porch so that she can watch the goings-on outside, but she scarcely opens her eyes and her breathing is still laboured.

'God bless you, little one,' she whispers in Angel's ear.

'I will be back before you know it,' says Angel brightly and plants a kiss on the sunken cheek.

With a couple of flat cakes and half a bottle of water in a plastic bag, Angel picks her way out of the barangay and onto the main road. It's eerily quiet. There are only a handful of vehicles and no shops are trading, but she can hear lots of banging and clattering going on as residents busily go about erecting shelter however they can.

She walks along the roadside past wrecked businesses. Those that were lucky enough to escape storm damage have since been broken into and looted. Windows have been smashed and doors broken down by people looking not only for food and water but also clothing and electrical goods to sell on the black market. Angel shakes her head.

She passes a shopping centre that only opened a few months ago. The front steps are littered with broken glass and items left behind by the thieves as they ran off with their spoils. She picks up a phone charger, lured by the thought of being able to call her mother, but then drops it again. It wouldn't be much use anyway because the old phone she and her father had was ruined in the storm.

A little curious, she walks up to one of the shops and peers in. There's not much stock left, just a couple of shirts askew on hangers, a single running shoe from one of those expensive American brands, and a pair of black sunglasses lying on the floor. They're half hidden under a display cabinet that has had its door broken open. The thieves probably didn't see them in their rush to get away. Angel picks them up. They're expensive and sleek looking, like the ones she's seen movie stars wearing on billboards. She looks around the abandoned store, almost tempted, then places them carefully on the counter top and leaves the shop.

The sun is peeking through dark clouds and it's hot and steamy. She can hear the regular drone of aircraft coming in and it comforts her to think that they're bringing help and provisions. There's purpose in her step as she heads towards the church.

Angel rounds a corner to see a long queue of people waiting patiently along the road. Ahead, soldiers are handing out bags of rice from an enormous trailer drawn by an equally large tractor. There are four soldiers standing on the top of a gigantic mound of rice sacks, rolling them one by one to a dozen or more soldiers below, who carefully load them onto the shoulders of the people in line. There's no pushing or shoving here. Although they're all no doubt very hungry, everyone is waiting their turn. She smiles as she passes and the people smile and wave back, even as the heavens open and the rain starts falling again.

Filipinos are a tough bunch, she thinks to herself. *And resilient.*

She rounds the next corner and comes upon yet another queue. People with buckets and containers of all shapes and sizes are lined up.

'What's going on?' she asks a young woman with a red plastic washtub and a tiny baby asleep in a sling on her back.

'It's a mobile water-treatment van,' she explains. 'They are pumping water into it from the city's water system and then purifying it so that it's safe to drink. There are a few of them around the city now.'

Angel is impressed. She realises this is the kind of equipment that's coming in on those big cargo planes. Whole families, from the elderly to small children, are sharing the job of carrying the heavy water containers home.

There are shelters here too. Schools have been turned into safe havens for people whose houses were ruined by the storm. She passes a high school building that looks full to bursting with families. Children wave at Angel from the upstairs windows and hoot happily when Angel waves back. She smiles to herself and wonders if her own school is also providing much-needed shelter.

The town hall is a welcome sight. Because it's on a hill there's little water damage and apart from a few broken windows the grand façade looks more or less as it did a few days before when Angel passed by in the jeepney with her mother and brothers. Several roof sheets have come off and they're lying on the muddy front lawn, where a number of aid agencies have set themselves up in tents and outbuildings, the staff distinctive in their hiking boots, cargo pants and cotton shirts. Many of them are Filipinos, but there are plenty of foreigners speaking in exotic languages, too.

Angel walks up the steps to the town hall and peeks inside. It's a long way from the cool, spacious interior that she imagined. The hall is being used as a base by the mayor and his staff as they coordinate the relief effort, and it's a hive of activity as workers bustle about. There are queues everywhere and the walls are lined with mountains of rice bags and packs of water that extend all the way up a large staircase.

Just outside the door Angel overhears a Filipino woman talking to a group of newly arrived workers still carrying their backpacks from the plane. They're all wearing USAID T-shirts.

'We've got shipments coming in all the time, as you would have seen at the airport. It's great that it's finally happening, but it's been very slow getting supplies out to the survivors.'

'How come?' asks one of the young aid workers.

'Everyone is negotiating with the government on how best to roll out the aid. It's complicated,' she sighs.

'Politics, eh?' says the young man.

She smiles ruefully. 'There's some debate over who's going to control things. It's time consuming. There are a lot of people here who need help so we need to get past the talking and get moving.'

Angel notices a queue nearby that seems to be for medical treatment, so she steps over to join it. Her various cuts and scrapes are painful and weeping and she needs to find a doctor to come and visit Mrs Reyes. She waits for what seems like hours in the beating sun. A man in a Red Cross hat hands out bottles of water and Angel takes one gratefully. A lady with 'UN' written on her blue T-shirt takes people's names and details.

'What's your date of birth?' she asks Angel. 'And where are your parents?'

Angel explains that she hasn't seen her parents since the storm.

'I hope to find my father today at the church.' She gestures down the hill, where the roof of Santo Niño is just visible.

The woman looks at her searchingly and nods. 'Okay,' she says. 'Go and look for your father, but if you don't find him there come back and see me and we will make sure you have somewhere safe to sleep tonight.'

Angel promises the woman and thanks her. She's getting close to the front of the line but the day is getting lost in this queuing, she realises, and she's desperate to find her father. She's about to give up and leave when a voice calls her name.

'Angel?'

She steps forward.

'Your turn.' A smiling woman in green shirt and trousers takes her hand and leads her into the medical tent, over to a counter covered in medicines and dressings. 'My name is Lucy. I'm from Manila and I just flew in this morning.' She smiles and gently picks up Angel's arm, which is scored with deep, ugly scratches. 'Now, what do we have here?'

One by one, Angel's cuts and abrasions are cleaned and dressed. The cut on her foot is the worst and Lucy is concerned about infection. She takes a lot of time cleaning it and finally bandages it tightly with a sticky dressing.

'It should have had stitches but I think it's too late now as it's partly healed,' she says with a sigh. 'You should try to come back here every day or two so we can change the dressing, otherwise it will get infected and make you sick. Do you understand?'

Angel nods. She winces as Lucy gives her an anti-biotic injection and another needle for tetanus.

'I think that's all we can do for now,' Lucy says.

'Oh please, there's one more thing. I have a friend, our neighbour, an old lady. She couldn't walk this far but she badly needs help. Can you come and see her?' Angel pleads.

Lucy looks at the long line of patients outside the tent.

'Not today. Come and see me early in the morning tomorrow and we will go then.'

Angel thanks her and takes a bottle of water and a couple of small packets of what look like hard cookies from a box nearby.

Two male aid workers are deep in conversation nearby and her ears prick up when she hears them mention Samar.

'Excuse me,' she says shyly. And then louder, when they don't respond: 'Excuse me?'

They stop mid-sentence and turn to her.

'Yes,' one man says brusquely.

'Do you know how bad the damage is on Samar? My mother and brothers are there. I can't find my father and I have no way of getting in touch with my family…' She trails off.

The men glance at each other.

'There is severe damage on Samar, especially along the coast. Where was your mother?'

'Near Basey,' Angel says. 'But a short distance inland.'

The two nod hopefully. 'Basey is very badly damaged, but if your family was away from the beach they may be okay.'

Angel doesn't know how to feel about this news. Severe damage! She thinks back to all the times she has visited her grandparents' place. Is it high enough and far enough away to have escaped the sea? What about the wind? Again she wishes that she had a phone to call her mother. She walks out the front of the town hall and stares at the placid ocean hundreds of metres away. It's hard to believe it can be so destructive.

She fixes her gaze on the tower of Santo Niño and begins to walk. It doesn't take her long even through the unrecognisable streets. Just before she reaches the church she encounters the bizarre sight of a police launch with its bold red sign 'PULISYA' in the middle of the road. It must have come to rest there after the water receded.

From the outside, it looks like the church has withstood the worst of the storm. The tower has lost its tiles and large parts of the roof have been torn off, but the structure is sound and most of the intricate stained-glass windows have survived. As she walks around the outside Angel sees the garden is a swirl of mud and rubbish, but it can be cleared and re-landscaped. It might have been so much worse. The cross has fallen from the steeple, but could be fixed, she reasons.

Quietly Angel steps through the back door and into the cavernous interior. She can smell the wax of burning candles and hear the low hum of prayers. A few dozen people are gathered and Mass is about to begin. She is not ready to join them yet.

Slowly Angel takes in the sight of the heavy wooden pews that have been swept aside like children's toys by the water, and left piled up against the far wall of the church. The floor is awash with mud. She walks into the open centre of the building, empty now, but where the pews should be, and looks up. The saints are still there catching the shafts of occasional weak sunlight on another overcast day. The sunbeams create a web of golden light across the ceiling where a couple of small birds flutter, the light bright on their wings.

Angel remembers the last time she was here, when her brothers chased the birds in this atrium while her mother spoke with the priest. It feels like so long ago.

Where are her little brothers now? Fear washes over her as she recalls that neither of them are strong swimmers yet. How she wishes she had spent more time practising in the water with them.

Father Jose begins his sermon by blessing those who have died and their loved ones left behind. Angel realises that most of those gathered for the service are weeping. She feels like weeping too.

At the back of the church there is a board covered in sheets of paper. Angel moves closer and sees that they are lists of the missing. She begins to read the hundreds and hundreds of names. She knows many of them – too many of them. They are people she and her family have met at church every Sunday for as long as she can remember. Fathers, mothers, brothers, sisters, babies…

She picks up a pen hanging on a string that is pinned to the noticeboard. At the bottom of the last list she carefully writes the names of Veronica, Cristian and Carlo. She puts down their ages, and when they were last seen. The pen hovers for a moment as Angel smothers a sob, then slowly adds Juan's name to the bottom of the list.

She is alone.

Ten

Outside the church Angel has no idea what to do next. She sinks to the ground and buries her face in her hands. 'Where are you? Where are you, Papa?' she moans as she gives in to her misery.

After a while she feels a gentle hand touching her head. Glancing up she sees a white robe through the blur of tears.

'Father?'

The priest takes her by the hands and lifts her to her feet. Close up she can see that his white robe is grubby and one lens of his thick glasses is cracked clean across. As always, the priest radiates peace and calm.

'Angel, I am so glad to see you safe. I hoped your mother was going to take you all to Samar?'

'I…I stayed with Papa…we didn't know the water would come…it swept him away…now I don't know where he is…' She is fighting to hold back the tears.

'Where have you looked for him?'

'I went back to the house and I waited. Then I came here, but I haven't seen him. Have you seen him?'

Father Jose shakes his head. 'What about your mother?'

'I don't know anything. I haven't heard. Our mobile phone is gone. There's no way to contact her...' Angel can hear herself babbling.

'You have experienced terrible things, child. You have felt awful fear. But you have been strong and resourceful. I'm proud of you.'

His words cheer her a little. He continues, 'Juan is a strong man, stronger than most. And he is a good swimmer. He would fight hard to survive.'

'Where can he be?'

'Have you tried the airport? Many of the injured have been taken there.'

'The airport!' Suddenly she has purpose again. 'How do I get there?'

Heavy trucks are rumbling back and forth, dropping supplies at the town hall and the church and returning to the airport. There is one outside the church now. The driver has just offloaded a crate of water bottles and Father Jose calls out to him.

'Ronaldo!'

The priest takes Angel by the hand and leads her over towards the truck.

'Ronaldo is one of our parishioners. A good man, very trustworthy,' he explains.

They reach the truck and he shakes the driver's hand. 'This is Angel. She needs to get to the airport. Can you take her?'

Ronaldo smiles down at her. 'The cab is full already,

I'm afraid. But if you don't mind riding in the back, you are welcome to come with us.'

'Thank you so much!' she says to him. 'And Father ...'

The priest is already on his way to his next task. 'Come back here afterwards; I will try to organise a phone. You and your family are in my prayers.'

Ronaldo helps Angel up onto the tray and she settles herself on a pile of empty sacks in the back corner.

'It will be slow going,' he warns her, 'but make sure you hang on to something as it will be very bumpy.'

The truck starts to pull away and Angel grabs tightly to the bars on the side. It feels good to be doing something and she nurses a glimmer of optimism. But as they slowly progress through the city, her spirits plummet again. It's a rolling scene of endless destruction as the truck slowly nudges its way along. In parts there is so much debris that it's piled up higher than a building. Broken timber and cement has been pushed aside, just enough for a single vehicle to pass through a kind of tunnel of rubble.

They pass the convention centre that juts out into the bay. There's damage to the façade and rubbish all around, but the building survived the onslaught and is now being used as an evacuation shelter for many hundreds of locals. Angel decides that if her father isn't at the airport, she will search there next.

When they reach the road to the airport she is stunned. The spit between the town and the terminal, once made up of a thriving collection of villages and roadside stalls, has borne the full brunt of the storm surge. It appears that the sea has washed straight over the top of the narrow strip of land, flattening everything in its path. Now and then she sees people perching high on the wreckage. They stare listlessly as she passes by.

Although Angel has never been on an aeroplane, she has been to the airport several times over the years to pick up her uncle and cousins when they visit from Malaysia. As they approach she sees that the main building has lost its roof, which is now spread around the carpark in pieces. The terminal itself is covered in mud and sludge washed in from the sea, which now laps softly on the other side of the main runway.

All around cargo planes and helicopters are landing and taking off. There are enormous pallets of rice bags sitting next to the terminal building, dozens of rows of army tents and a few big, noisy generators. Filipino military and soldiers from different countries are busy giving directions in strange languages and accents, loading and unloading planes and moving trolleys loaded with goods marked 'Australian Aid', 'USAID' or 'Gift from the people of Thailand', or Singapore or Japan.

Then Angel sees all the displaced people. Hundreds of them squashed up against the main gate that leads onto the tarmac. Clearly there are entire families waiting to fly out; elderly, injured and small children, too. They seem to have been waiting a long time. Bodies are slumped in despair, babies cry feebly in the sticky heat. She can understand why they would want to get out of here. Many would be fleeing to relatives in the nearby city of Cebu or further to Manila. With their homes and livelihoods destroyed, there is no reason to stay.

All at once there is a commotion as the engine of one of the cargo planes starts powering up to take off. A few dozen people who have been cleared to board set out across the tarmac carrying plastic bags and children. The crowd surges against the gate and a handful of people slip through. Angel watches as a man and a woman carrying a baby are forcibly pushed back through the gate by the row of soldiers on the tarmac. They drag the gate closed again and hold their positions, arms folded and faces impassive as the desperate people wail with grief and frustration. It's horrible to see. She turns her head away as her truck slows to a stop. Four aid workers climb out of the cab and stride away.

Ronaldo jumps out and helps her down from the tray.

'I have to leave you, I'm afraid,' he says kindly. 'There's treated water and food here if you're willing to queue for it.' He points at a long line of people holding jerry cans on the other side of the airport.

'Do you know where the hospital tent is?' she asks.

He indicates a strange structure about a hundred metres from the airport, made up of what looks like a group of giant pop-up dome tents. 'Australians,' he says with a smile. 'They brought the whole hospital in on one of their aircraft. Quite amazing. It's full of medical supplies and it even has two operating theatres, although I'm not sure if they're up and running yet.'

Angel thanks him for the lift.

'I'll be heading back to the town hall in a few hours if you want a ride. The truck will be full but you can ride with me in the cab if you don't mind being squashed in with some other passengers.'

Angel wants to ask if there would be room for her father, too, but she stops herself. There's only a slim chance that he is here and if he is in the hospital, there's no telling how injured he might be. With a heavy heart, Angel strikes out towards the hospital across the churned-up landscape.

Inside, she's feeling a whirlwind of emotions. Is this it? Is this when she will finally be reunited with her father? What if he is badly injured? How will she cope with seeing him like that? Even worse, what if he isn't here at all? *Then I will have to try the convention centre and if he isn't there, then...*

Her fingers creep up to the pearl necklace tucked beneath her shirt. She runs her thumb over the smooth surface and pictures her father, bursting with pride when he gave it to her only days before.

As she draws closer she can see that the hospital is made up of a whole lot of long, domed structures, like caterpillars lying next to each other in a row. They're not quite tents, not quite buildings. Something in between.

As she expected, there is a growing queue of people outside the entrance: some have rough, homemade splints and crutches and bloody bandages. Others who are unable to walk are lying on crude pallets. A doctor is examining them, one by one, directing them this way or that.

A woman with a blonde ponytail wearing a pale blue hospital uniform hurries past carrying what looks like a giant box of bandages.

Angel darts forward. 'Excuse me, can you please help me?'

The woman looks at her kindly. 'I'm sorry, sweetie, but you'll have to join the line and wait your turn.'

'I'm not sick. I've been treated already,' insists Angel. 'I'm looking for my father. They said he might be here. Please, I need to find him.'

The woman stops and takes in Angel's clean bandages and her young face full of desperate hope.

'Come with me then,' she says quickly. 'Stay close and don't touch anything.'

Together they enter the first tent-like structure. It's like a proper medical clinic with steel equipment, trolleys laden with supplies and staff moving around purposefully.

Seated behind a small folding desk is a much younger woman, squinting over a messy pile of papers and a small laptop computer.

'Sorry to interrupt you, Leanne, but this young lady needs some help finding her dad. Can I leave her with you? Got to get these to post-op ASAP.'

The young woman glances up from her work impatiently, but then she sees Angel and her expression softens.

'Sure. I'll take over.'

'Thank you,' stutters Angel to the retreating woman's ponytail.

'Good luck!' she calls over her shoulder as she disappears back out the door.

'I'm Leanne,' says the young nurse. 'And you are?'

'My name is Angel.'

'Nice to meet you, Angel.'

Even though her heart is thudding in her chest, Angel smiles shyly. 'My father is called Juan. I haven't seen him since the storm.'

'Do you have any other family?' Leanne asks carefully.

'My mother and brothers went to Samar. I can't get in touch with them. Nothing is working.'

'Yes, I know. Lots of work's going into getting communications up again,' Leanne sighs. 'It's a big problem.'

'My father is a good swimmer. He's a fisherman. He knows how to survive ...' Angel trails off weakly.

'Okay then. Well, we have treated quite a few people already. Some are being moved to proper hospitals, but getting them there isn't easy so we have a bit of a queue.' She indicates her pile of papers. 'The doctors are writing patient details down and I'm transferring it all to a spreadsheet, but as you can see, I've a long way to go.'

'Oh please, can you have a look, please?' Angel's voice wobbles as the worry and tension starts to overwhelm her.

'I think we can do better than that.' Leanne steps out from behind the desk. 'I'm going to take you straight into recovery and we'll see if we can find him. Do you think you can do that?'

Angel nods quickly.

'There are some very sick people in there. Are you okay with that?'

'I'm okay with that,' Angel replies firmly, though she's not at all sure that she is.

'Now tell me what your dad looks like. How old is he?'

'He is forty-one years old.'

'And what is his build? Is he short or tall? Large or small?'

Angel tries to picture how other people would see her father.

'He is maybe a head taller than me. And he is thin but very muscly. And oh!' She suddenly remembers something that sets Juan apart. 'He has a white streak in his hair. He's had it since he was a teenager. He says it makes him look distinguished.' She smiles at the memory and her throat aches from trying not to cry.

Leanne raises her eyebrows. 'Right!' she snaps abruptly. 'Follow me.' They push through thick plastic doors and immediately Angel's nostrils are filled with the sharp tang of disinfectant. The narrow space is lined either side with camp beds, every one of them occupied by a patient. Some of them are unconscious or sleeping and heavily bandaged. A few are hooked up to softly humming machines with blinking red lights. Apart from the occasional beeping it's eerily quiet after the hustle and bustle outside.

They begin to move down the centre. Angel glances sideways and sees a woman with thick curly hair fanned out on the pillow. One of her arms rests on the blanket beside her and the other is swathed in bandages but Angel can see the blood soaking through the white cloth.

Leanne catches her eye.

'There's a chance we can save her arm,' she says quietly. 'We have two operating theatres that should be up and running in the next couple of days.'

Angel bows her head and focuses on Leanne's feet as the young nurse leads her on. They continue right down to the end and Leanne stops at the last bed on the left.

'He came in this morning. One of our first patients. He has a badly broken arm and has had a terrible crack on the head so we're keeping him here. Unfortunately, he hasn't said anything yet.'

Angel is almost too frightened to look. Reluctantly, she lifts her gaze to the face on the pillow. One side of the head is covered in bandage, but a thick black thatch of hair is still exposed showing the familiar white streak flaring up from the side part.

'Papa,' breathes Angel and she steps in closer.

His eyes flicker open and rest on his daughter as the tears finally spill over and roll down her face.

'You are here,' he whispers.

Eleven

Angel hasn't let go of Juan's hand since she found him an hour ago. One of his arms is in plaster and he has suffered a bad concussion, but there is no permanent damage. They have both shed tears of relief, and now Angel begins to tell her father of her miraculous escape.

'I saw her!' exclaims Juan when Angel describes her rooftop rescue. 'I caught a glimpse of Mrs Reyes and I pushed you up through the water with all my strength.'

'She held on to me, Papa, and she never let go. For hours and hours. She saved me.'

'Thank God she was there,' sighs Juan.

'And look, Papa, I still have my pearl!'

'You see? I stayed with you, like I said I would.'

'What about you, Papa? What happened to you when the water filled the house?'

As he recounts his story, Juan fixes his gaze on the ceiling of the tent, as if picturing the traumatic scene from days before.

'I pushed you up but the sea snatched me back and I was sucked down. It was a whirlpool: spinning over and over, bouncing off the walls and the furniture. I have never felt so helpless. I couldn't breathe. I tried to find the door or a window but I was thrown around so fast. And then I knew I had to get out the same way as you, through the roof, so I swam up and I managed to get a breath or two. But I couldn't find the opening, just timber and iron. And I wished, oh how I wished that I hadn't built my walls so strong and my roof so sturdy!'

They both laugh weakly at that.

'Finally the whole roof came off in one piece and I was dragged out with it. I was so confused, so frightened, being pulled along at such a speed. No control. A car floated past me. A CAR! Then a wooden pallet floated by and I threw myself onto it with the last bit of my strength. Like a big clumsy raft it smashed into things and bounced around in the black swirling water. I clung on for my life.'

Juan pauses for a moment and winces at the awful memory of it.

'I called out for you, my Angel. I screamed your name. I thought the storm had taken you. And then the pallet smashed into a building, exploding into pieces and I was thrown onto the rooftop where I passed out. And that's where I woke up.'

He lies there, eyes closed, taking deep, calming breaths.

'Shall I leave you to sleep, Papa?' Angel enquires timidly. Juan grips her hand tighter. 'No, no, not yet.

I have to tell you the rest. You must hear this! When I came to, I was on the top of a two-storey building. My head was throbbing and sticky with blood. My arm was terribly painful. I realised that I was on top of a bakery – you know the one beside the jeans shop? More than a kilometre from home. That's how far the water had swept me! When I stood up I was dizzy and I nearly passed out again from the pain, but I had to get home. I had to find you. So I climbed down through the building and started walking.'

'How did you do it, Papa?' marvels Angel. 'How did you manage?'

'I really don't know. It was all a blur. I cradled my bad arm with my good arm and put one foot in front of the other until I reached the shore. And that's where I found it.'

'Found what?'

'My bangka! It was still there; upside down, but it looked like it wasn't badly damaged.'

'I saw it too,' marvels Angel. 'I couldn't believe it had survived.'

Juan is getting agitated and a sense of urgency is creeping into his raspy voice. 'Here's the thing, though. If the boat is still seaworthy – and I think that it is – then we can take it across to Samar and find your mother and brothers. They must be frantic. We need to let them know that we are both alright.'

Angel does not have the heart to tell him that Samar suffered severe storm damage as well and there are no guarantees that they have survived.

'First you need rest,' Angel says evenly. 'You need to regain your strength.'

Juan is starting to drift off to sleep. 'We have to find a new engine and motor across to Samar. Soon we will all be together again...'

Angel holds his hand for a few minutes more, then stands and stretches her stiff limbs. Leanne is watching her from further down the room where she is tending a patient. She beckons her over.

'I'm so glad you've found each other. Happy endings are thin on the ground at the moment.'

'I can't thank you enough,' says Angel.

'Thank the good Samaritan who found him. He came across your father slumped against a boat. He must have passed out from the pain and blood loss and he'd been lying there for some time. This young man looked after him overnight and then somehow managed to get him to the town hall, where they treated him as best they could and brought him here this morning.'

'Wow,' says Angel in awe. 'Do you know his name?'

'The medic who brought him in just told me the story. No name. Situations like this can bring out the very best in people.'

'And the very worst,' says Angel softly, thinking of the looters who broke in to Issy's house. 'How soon can Papa be released?'

Leanne touches Angel lightly on the arm. 'Your father has a very bad concussion. He will be alright, I think, but he won't be going anywhere for a couple of days.'

Angel nods silently. The joy of being reunited with Juan evaporates as she is jarred back to the reality of their situation.

'Do you have somewhere to stay?' asks Leanne. 'Somewhere safe where you can wait until your father is well enough to look after you?'

Angel nods again. She can't trust herself to speak in case she bursts into tears again. What is she going to do now? How is she going to get to Samar on her own?

Leanne's voice is full of concern. 'If not, I know they are setting up safe centres at the town hall for children who haven't got…' she hesitates '…for children who can't find their families yet.'

She may be at a loss about what to do next, but Angel knows that she can't spend the next few days waiting around for her father to regain his health. If Juan can't do it, then somehow she must find her mother and brothers herself.

'No, I'll be fine,' she assures Leanne. 'I am staying with my friend's family at Barangay 18. They have plenty of food and water. I'll be safe there.' She deliberately exaggerates the last bit to avoid more questions.

The nurse is clearly relieved. 'Okay, well I think you should head back there now. It will be dark soon and your father is heavily sedated. He will sleep for several hours at least.'

'I will come back to visit him when I can,' says Angel. 'But please let him know that I heard what he said and I will do my best. He will understand what that means.'

Angel looks back at her sleeping father, then she walks out of the recovery room and through the busy hospital reception area. Outside the light is beginning to fade from the already gloomy sky. Far in the distance she can see the truck that brought her here. The tray is fully loaded and there are people getting into the front cab.

'Ronaldo!' she shouts. 'Ronaldo, wait for me! I'm coming too!'

When they arrive back at the church, Ronaldo offers to take her to the town hall where there is food and shelter, but Angel thanks him and says no, there is something she needs to do here first.

She walks straight through the front entrance of Santo Niño and down to the noticeboards at the back. Already there are dozens of names that have been added to the lists of the missing since she was here earlier in the day. Angel picks up the pen on a string and carefully crosses out Juan's name and writes next to it: 'Found safe'. She stares at the names of her mother and brothers. Finding out what has happened to them is her number one priority now. Her thoughts are interrupted by the sound of a motor running somewhere nearby. Does this mean the electricity is back on? She rushes towards the back of the church. Just outside, set up on an area that has been cleared of rubbish, is a large, rattly generator. She runs over to Father Jose, who is standing next to it talking to a small group of people.

'No one could charge their phones to contact family members with the power off,' he explains, 'so I thought we could help by bringing in a generator from Cebu. It took a bit of organising because of transport issues, but we did it! The network is still not completely fixed but at least this means some people might be able to get a call through. The church piggy bank will be stretched for a while but I think it's a good use of our funds, don't you?'

Angel sees there must be at least ten power boards neatly placed side by side on a cement ledge by the machine and they're all full of charging phones.

'What a great idea!' exclaims one of the onlookers.

'And the added bonus is that we now have light at the church at night.' The priest sees Angel and waves her over. She quickly fills him in on Juan's situation.

'Wonderful. Now we just need to find the rest of your family. Do you know your mother's phone number?'

Angel nods. 'But I don't have a phone, Father.'

'Wait here,' he says, and disappears into a small office at the back of the church building. He emerges waving a phone and a charger on a long cable and hands it to her.

'I've had this old spare sitting in a drawer for years. It's no smart phone, but it should be okay for making calls if you can get a signal. I've charged it up already for you. Hopefully it has some credit left on it. Good luck!' And he swishes away again, the hem of his robe dragging in the mud.

Angel gazes in wonder at the chunky old push-button mobile in her hand.

She carefully unplugs it and stows the charger in her plastic bag. Around her, people are coming to retrieve their phones before they find a place to sleep for the night and there's an air of something close to camaraderie as strangers and friends run into each other at the power boards. Some tear their phones from the sockets and immediately start dialling, weeping with joy when the call is answered, or gulping in disappointment when it isn't. It's hit and miss.

Some call family overseas or in Manila, for the first time since the storm. There's palpable joy and much laughter as first contact is made with those who've heard nothing for days from their relatives. What a difference a phone call can make.

'We are all alive, Mama,' a young woman says, cradling a baby and a toddler and smiling as she weeps with the phone to her ear. 'We have lost everything, we are hungry, we are tired but we are all alive.' She laughs into the phone as the children wriggle in her arms. A young man – her husband, Angel guesses – takes the baby and cuddles the little boy, tickling him under the armpits until he giggles in delight. Angel grins. Happiness is still here. Will she find it too, on the end of the line?

She turns the phone over and over in her hands. The battery is full. She can make the call but she can't bring herself to do it. What if the news is bad? How will she cope with it alone if the worst has happened to Veronica and the boys? And what of her beloved grandparents?

Her stomach clenches, but she has no choice. She has to know. Slowly she enters Veronica's number on the old keypad, double-checking that it's correct, then she presses send and puts the phone to her ear. Several seconds pass as the connection stalls and then goes through, but the dull insistent beep tells her that the phone she is calling is turned off. She presses 'End' on the keypad and swallows her disappointment. Perhaps there's no signal yet on Samar. Or maybe they have no way of charging the phone? Perfectly reasonable explanations. Angel refuses to let it get her down.

I will try again later, she says to herself and puts the phone in her pocket. Her hand is shaking a little and she realises she needs to get some food and water and somewhere safe to sleep. She can't afford to get sick – her family is depending on her.

Slowly she walks out of the churchyard and up the hill to the town hall, where the queues are still winding out of the makeshift medical clinic. The front lawn is now covered in tents and marquees where the staff of various aid agencies are locked in planning meetings about the logistics of the clean-up or distributing food, water and medicine to the survivors.

Angel joins a line where people are waiting for food. Volunteers are passing out white polystyrene boxes. Angel has no idea what's in them but she doesn't care. She's so hungry she would eat anything. She wolfs down the rice and meat inside, barely tasting it. Her whole body starts to droop as the efforts of the day take their toll. A woman handing out water bottles comes over to her and says, 'There's a children's shelter over there,' indicating a building a little further down the hill.

Angel thanks her and makes her way there slowly. Inside, small battery lamps cast a warm, yellow glow over rows of mats laid down neatly, about half of them already occupied by sleeping children. A volunteer gives her a light blanket and thin pillow and tells her she can sleep where she likes.

Angel finds a banig in the corner and lies down under the blanket. She is asleep before her head hits the pillow.

Twelve

Angel wakes early. She folds her blanket and tiptoes around the sleeping children and out into the grey dawn light. She turns on the phone and keys in Veronica's number, but it is still turned off. Angel tries not to think about all of the bad things that could have happened to her mother and brothers. She's still clinging to the hope that the lack of contact is a simple case of the phones and electricity being off in Samar.

The makeshift camp is already stirring as she walks up to the town hall, taking in the view of the silvery sea from the top of the hill before heading into the surgery tent. She searches for the medic who promised to come with her to see Mrs Reyes and finds Lucy sorting dressings ahead of the morning rush.

'Ah Angel,' she grins. 'I wondered if you'd come back.'

'Here I am, ready to go,' says Angel eagerly.

'Okay, we will go and see your friend, but first let me take a look at your foot.'

Once Angel's foot is cleaned again, Lucy shoulders

a large bag of medical supplies and they head down towards the road where they should be able to catch a lift.

There are a few television cameras around filming the recovery effort. The camera crews are wearing caps and T-shirts showing what channel they're from. Some are from familiar Filipino TV channels; others are foreigners with CNN and BBC and ABC logos on their cameras and clothing.

Most of the journalists look hot, tired and bedraggled. Some appear to be camping in tents on the lawn. For the first time Angel considers that Tacloban's terrible tragedy has grabbed world attention. She's not sure that's a good thing; she wants the world to know that there is much more to her city than the death and destruction of Yolanda.

Down the hill soldiers and clean-up crews have suddenly arrived en masse and are chainsawing fallen trees and piling debris onto the backs of trucks. They're grouped into teams, wearing coloured T-shirts printed with things like 'Yolanda clean-up crew' or 'I love Tacloban'. Angel is pleased to see them at work. Here in the centre of the city at least, there are big efforts being made to return to some sort of normality.

Two trucks are standing by to begin the clean-up elsewhere. Lucy goes up to one of the drivers. 'Are you going anywhere near Barangay 18?' she enquires.

'Not me,' he replies. 'But he is.'

The other driver is happy to take them to Issy's place on the back of his truck. Minutes later they are on their way. Angel is looking forward to seeing Mrs Reyes again, especially now that she can share the good news about her father. She is so glad to be able to repay the old lady in some small way by bringing her medical help.

The big truck jolts through the city's devastated streets. It's still a mess but already Angel can see signs of progress. There are workers on cherry pickers repairing powerlines and phone towers, residents hammering sheets of iron back onto damaged roofs and clean-up crews sweeping debris from the roads. As far as the eye can see, though, there are mountains of rubble. It's difficult to imagine the city will ever recover from this.

The big truck grinds to a halt at the end of Issy's lane. Angel and Lucy jump down, thanking the driver for the ride and waving as the truck lurches away. Angel leads them down the cluttered alley, climbing over sheets of loose tin and boards that have yet to be cleared. The mud has begun to dry so the churned-up mess of grass and stones and dirt is hard and unyielding. The plank across to Issy's front door is still in place and they step across it gingerly onto the porch.

'Is anybody here? It's Angel. I'm back!'

Issy bursts from the house, her arms flung wide.

'Angel, thank goodness you're okay. We were so worried!' She hugs Angel tightly.

'I'm sorry I didn't get back last night as I promised, but I found Papa!'

Danilo and Maria emerge from the house, their faces drawn with anxiety.

'Finally!' says Maria as she embraces her. They are clearly relieved to see Angel and hear her news, but there is a strange nervousness, too.

'This is Lucy,' Angel says. 'She's a medic and she's come to see Mrs Reyes.'

Issy glances at her parents and they exchange looks.

Suddenly, Angel knows.

'Mrs Reyes?' she calls.

She turns to her friend. 'Issy?'

Issy looks stricken as she grasps Angel's hands. 'I'm so sorry, Angel. It was just after you left. She was so tired and she fell asleep. When I went to wake her she had passed away.'

'It must have been her heart, Angel,' Danilo says gently. 'We knew she wasn't well. It was all too much for her.'

Angel slumps down on the cement porch and the tears come quickly.

'She saved me,' Angel sobs. 'I was bringing help but I was too late.'

Lucy crouches down in front of her.

'It's not your fault, Angel,' she says quietly. 'You did your very best. Mrs Reyes would be the first to say that.'

'I should have been faster,' Angel sniffles. 'I should have brought you straight back with me.'

Lucy shrugs wearily. 'It may have helped. It may not have. Heart problems are difficult to treat, especially in circumstances like this. You did what you could, Angel. Never forget that.'

Lucy stands and addresses the others. 'I'm so sorry

I couldn't help, but I must get back. Please let me check all of you over before I go.'

She dresses their cuts and scratches and gives each of them a tetanus and antibiotic injection. She hugs Angel, who has remained slumped on the porch and whispers, 'Stay strong.'Then she heads out to the road to find a lift back to the town hall.

After a while, Angel picks herself up and walks a small distance down the lane. Issy's family means well but she needs to be alone to gather her thoughts. Outside a ruined house, a small car has come to rest. Angel sits down on its battered hood and stares glumly at the surroundings. She had been so energised at finding her father alive, but now her fears for the rest of her family crowd in and the death of Mrs Reyes hangs heavily over everything.

A little boy of two or three is squatting amid the rubble on the other side of the lane. He's arranging small pieces of concrete in a row and chatting away to himself. Angel realises that he's playing some sort of game. Even with carnage all around, children will always play, thinks Angel.

The next moment she's on her feet hurrying back to Issy's house. The faded teddy that she found on the beach a few days before is propped on the windowsill, where she'd left it to dry after washing it in a bucket of rainwater. It looks a lot better now and the tiny bell around the teddy's neck even tinkles softly. She brushes it off and takes it back to the boy in the lane.

'Hello there. Look what I found!' she says. 'This

little guy needs a new person to take care of him. Can you help?'

The boy regards her with astonishment. She hands him the teddy and he lets out a shriek of delight. His skinny little arms hug the toy close and his face is a picture of happiness as he runs off down the lane. 'Mama! Mama!' he shouts. 'I have a bear!'

Justin has come up behind her. 'That's a pretty cool thing to do,' he says.

'What can I say?' she shrugs. 'The bear needed a home.'

She settles down again on the hood of the car.

Justin asks, 'May I?' When she nods he sits down next to her. A week ago, it's the last thing that either of them would think of doing, but now everything is different.

'I'm sorry about Mrs Reyes,' he says gruffly.

'Mmm-hmm,' she responds.

'And I'm sorry about telling you off the other night.'

'I *was* pretty stupid...'

'Yes, but you're right. I would have done exactly the same thing.'

'Okay. Apology accepted.'

'What are you going to do now?'

'I need to find my mum and my brothers. I need to get to Samar.' She pulls out the phone again and dials her mother's number.

'No signal,' she tells him as she puts it away again.

'I'm not surprised,' says Justin. 'I've heard it's worse than here. I hear the bridge is okay but the roads to get to it are blocked, and who knows what it's like on the other side.'

'I know. The only sure way to get there is by sea.'

'Every boat in Tacloban was destroyed by the storm,' says Justin regretfully.

'Not every boat,' says Angel, and she tells him about Juan's bangka.

'So the boat is sound,' Justin says slowly. 'It's just the engine that's the problem?'

'That's what Papa said.'

Justin jumps down from the car and turns to Angel with a light in his eyes. 'I have an idea.'

Thirteen

Angel and Justin re-enter the house. Seeing them together Issy raises her eyebrows and follows as they stride purposefully through to the back courtyard, where Danilo and Maria are clearing out some of the mess.

Justin puts their plan to his parents in an urgent, persuasive tone.

'If it doesn't work then we'll come straight back here, won't we, Angel?' argues Justin.

'Absolutely!'

Maria is standing with her arms crossed and a stubborn frown on her face. Danilo is looking at his son with a strange mixture of pride and concern.

'It's too dangerous. You're too young. Tell him, Danilo!' protests Maria.

Her husband considers for a moment. 'Justin has been out on the boats many times, my darling. He's been helping me for years and in ordinary circumstances I would be more than confident he could take a boat to Samar and back by himself.'

'Oh, you're a great help!' Maria retorts.

'However,' continues Danilo, 'the conditions are totally different now. The sea is full of dangers and obstacles; only the most skilled driver would be able to navigate through.'

'And, kids, there will still be bodies out there in the water,' adds Maria.

Angel and Justin look at each other grimly.

Angel speaks up slowly. 'We'll find one of Papa's fishing friends to take us. Surely some of them will still be in the neighbourhood.'

'And I bet there'd be at least one who needs to get to Samar and hasn't got a boat to get him there. They'll be jumping at the chance!' says Justin.

Everyone turns to Maria. She's running out of arguments but she hasn't given up yet. 'I'm sure your mother wouldn't let you go.'

'But that's just it!' bursts out Angel. 'I might not have a mother if she doesn't get help soon. She could be ill or badly injured, and they are saying that conditions are even worse over there. Please let us go – this may be her only hope!'

That's done it. Maria's arms drop loosely to her sides.

'You have to promise me you won't make the trip on your own. And you stay together at all times.'

'Got it,' Angel and Justin say together.

'And wait until the morning to set out,' Danilo adds. 'Conditions will be better then.'

The two teenagers exchange a glance and then nod in agreement. Their rescue mission is going ahead!

That evening, the little group holds a simple memorial for Mrs Reyes in the front of the house. Earlier, Issy managed to assemble a small altar with a statuette of Mary and Jesus, candles, plastic flowers and woven reeds. Mrs Reyes was carefully bathed and wrapped in some colourful fabrics that Maria was saving for Issy. Then she was placed in a body bag from one of the Red Cross trucks. Danilo wouldn't let them take her away to one of the mass graves for those killed in the storm. He's on a mission to contact her family, find her a decent coffin and then hold a proper burial.

They light some candles, say a few prayers and Maria leads them in singing 'The Lord Is My Shepherd' and then the famous ballad 'Hindi Kita Malilimutan, I Will Never Forget You'.

At the end, Angel whispers, 'Mrs Reyes loved that song.'

Issy squeezes her hand and whispers back, 'We will *never* forget her.'

At dawn, the family is up and Maria gives the travellers some packets of peanuts and two precious bottles of water. Angel and Justin say their farewells and turn down the lane towards the waterfront, which they have decided should be the quickest way to get to Angel's house. There hasn't been much cleaning up down here close to the sea though. It looks much the same as it did when Angel passed through with Mrs Reyes just four days ago. There are still mountains of rubble and trash everywhere. Some people have made makeshift shelters amid the debris, using broken bits of roof and timber, but others are still sheltering beneath plastic tarpaulins.

Here the concerted effort to collect the dead is obvious. At one point they pass a row of white body bags emblazoned with the distinctive Red Cross logo. Angel can't help but think of Mrs Reyes and the fact that they can't even give her a proper burial.

The two of them make much better time than Angel did on her journey out with the old woman. They trudge along at a decent pace until they round the curve in the shoreline. Then Angel sees her father's little bangka still untouched and upside down in the mud. It looks in bad shape but when they get up close and Justin does a swift inspection, he says, 'Your father is right. This hull is seaworthy.'

Angel eyes it doubtfully. It's going to be a big job to even turn it over, let alone get it back into the water.

'First things first. Let's see if we can find an engine.'

Yesterday, when Angel mentioned the bangka, Justin had remembered his friend Nelson, who lives in an apartment above his father's mechanic's shop not far from Angel's house. The two friends liked to hang around the small tin shed on the roof where Nelson's father worked refurbishing old engines that he would sell at a reduced price. Angel listens now as Justin explains how the engines are stored in a heavy steel cabinet.

Angel follows Justin inland for about a hundred

metres. He keeps pausing to work out where he is, and eventually he points ahead to a huddle of shops and declares triumphantly, 'There it is!'

Although the building is still intact, the doors of the mechanic's shop have been torn open and the inside fully stripped of anything useful. Angel guesses people have been in here looking for tools. But the metal stairs to the apartment are still in place and they climb to the upper floor where they find the inside has also been looted and abandoned.

Justin's face is ashen as he surveys his friend's former home.

'Nelson said that he and his family were evacuating to Cebu to stay with relatives. They are not going to be happy coming home to this.'

The ladder that used to access the manhole in the roof is nowhere to be seen. The two of them drag a large table over and Justin steadies a chair on top of it. Then he unhooks the latch and pops open the manhole, pulling himself up easily through the ceiling. Moments later his head appears through the opening and his hand reaches down to Angel.

'Come on up. You've got to see this!'

The roof is almost entirely clear of objects. The force of the wind has swept everything away except for a large steel trunk chained down by heavy metal rings embedded in the cement.

'Is that it?' Angel exclaims.

'Incredible, isn't it?' says Justin, heaving the heavy lid open.

There are three boat engines inside the trunk and Justin immediately focuses on one that Angel can see is very similar to her father's.

'Do you think it works?' she asks Justin.

'It looks alright to me,' he answers as he examines the casing, then points excitedly at a slip of paper attached to the bottom with a rubber band. He rips it off and holds it out to her. 'It's got the owner's name and the cost of repairs. That means the job was finished and this engine was waiting to be collected. We're in luck!'

'What about Nelson's dad?' Angel asks. 'Will he mind?'

Justin says, 'I think he'd want to help you find your family.' Angel smiles at his kindness.

It takes them another precious hour to get the engine back to Juan's bangka. It's almost as heavy as Angel, which probably explains why the looters haven't taken it already. It's so unwieldy that they have to lower it down from the roof with a sort of sling made out of seat belts from the workshop. Then, suspending it from a long steel pole, they carry it between them across their shoulders. They also take a hammer, a spanner and a screwdriver from the trunk.

It's slow going and they don't reach the boat until mid-morning. Angel can't help missing her father's strength in this situation. She feels a pang of guilt that he might be expecting her to visit today.

'Now we need to get her upright,' sighs Justin. He gives the boat an experimental shove but it's stuck fast in the mud and barely moves. He looks around for help but everyone looks busy collecting or repairing things.

'If only we had a tractor,' he laments.

'Yeah right,' she laughs.

They sit down and look across the water at Samar. It seems so close but it may as well be on another planet.

'I'm going to swap the engines over,' says Justin. 'It's easier when it's upside down anyway.'

He begins to dismantle the waterlogged engine on the bangka with the tools from the trunk. At first Angel watches, but after a while she wanders off down the waterfront, checking out the damage to their neighbours' houses. It's all much the same along this stretch. Most of the buildings have been knocked over and those that haven't lost their roofs have been completely flooded. There's little left to salvage.

Some of the neighbours recognise her and wave from wherever they're hammering, nailing or collecting items from their damaged homes. Then she meets one of her father's fishermen friends. He is pleased to hear that Juan made it through. She tells him of her family's situation and that she and her friend are trying to fix the boat so that they can get to Samar.

'My wife and children are in Manila,' he explains. 'I thought we could come back and rebuild, but as you can see, there's nothing to come back for.' He indicates his former home, pulverised beyond repair.

'Here,' he says, going to a crate that he has been filling with a few salvageable items. 'You'll be needing some fuel. It's very hard to come by because the service stations have been damaged and the pumps aren't working. There's a black market already and the prices are crazy, so people are siphoning it out of the fuel tanks of abandoned vehicles.'

He hands her two screw-top glass bottles containing amber liquid.

'That should be enough to get you there and back,' he says. 'It's not much use to me. My boat was wrecked. Take it and I wish you and your friend the best of luck.'

Angel is warmed by his generosity. She thanks him profusely and starts back to the bangka.

'Could do with some help here!' Justin calls out to her. He has loosened the old engine and now he needs to lower it to the ground. Angel places the bottles of fuel in a broken basket lying nearby and hurries over to assist. The procedure is more awkward than heavy, but Justin seems to know what he is doing. He steps back to survey his work. 'It's ready to take the new engine,' he tells her. 'We're going to need fuel though. That's going to be difficult.'

Angel picks up the bottles from the basket and holds them out to him.

Justin grins. 'Wow! I'm not even going to ask how you managed that. Now we just have to work out how to turn this boat over.'

There's a loud revving and they see a truck inching along the road that runs by the water. Three men are in front of it, tossing rubbish out of the way so that the truck can pass, but it's slow going. The driver waves and smiles at the two teenagers. Then he drops the truck to an idle and leans out the window.

'Looks like you could do with some help?'

'Oh yes, please,' replies Angel.

'Well, it's going to take us all day to make a path through this mess, so we may as well do something useful…'

He drives the truck over and the clean-up crew attach some thick steel cables to the boat. The vessel is winched up, up, up onto its end and lowered down so that it's settled the right way up. Now that it's been flipped and is close to the water's edge, the new engine is lifted into the boat and fastened securely in place. Then everyone grabs hold and they start to inch the boat slowly to the lip of the cement wall. The truck driver lets out the cable while they keep the little boat level and upright until finally it plops into the shallow water.

Everyone claps and cheers as the bangka bobs about in the sea. So far so good. 'Salamat, salamat!' say Angel and Justin and the clean-up crew wishes them 'Swerte, good luck!' before they head off to resume their slow progress clearing the road.

It's a sunny afternoon, still steamy with a few clouds. They drink thirstily from the water bottles and crunch on peanuts. The sea is flat and a pale, milky blue. Again Angel reflects on how changeable the ocean is. Deadly one minute, idyllic the next.

Justin licks his lips nervously. 'I guess we better try it out then.'

They climb into the boat and Justin attempts to start the engine. It almost kicks, but there's a deafening rattle and it peters out. He fetches his tools and tinkers for a while.

Angel is content to sit in the prow while Justin does his repairs. 'When did you learn to do this? I thought you were all about maths and study.'

'Ah well,' smiles Justin. 'This is all part of my master plan. One day I'm going to run a fleet of fishing boats. It's going to be huge – the most successful business in Tacloban – but I'll need to be able to do all the numbers and the accounting. I'm going to be my own boss.'

Angel is impressed. 'Why do you know about fixing boats then?'

'A good boss needs to understand every aspect of the business inside out, don't you think? That way, my employees will respect me as one of them.'

Angel had no idea that Issy's brother was such an entrepreneur. Like her, he has been making plans for his future from a young age. Underneath the swagger he is hardworking and highly motivated.

Lifting her gaze she sees a big black seabird wheeling in the sky overhead. She's sure it's the same one she's seen before and is oddly comforted to think that somehow it survived the storm and made its way back here.

The quiet is shattered as the engine finally sputters into life. Justin revs it hard, concentrating until he's satisfied with its rhythm.

'Okay, we're in business,' he says. 'Let's do this.'

'What about your mother?' protests Angel suddenly. 'We promised her we'd find an experienced fisherman to take us over.'

'See any experienced fishermen here?' He indicates the now almost deserted beach. 'Come on, we can do this. We don't need adults to help us, we've come this far.'

Angel is nervous about the journey across and what they might find in Samar, but it's the only way to learn what has happened to her mother and brothers.

Fourteen

Angel sits in the prow and grips the edge of the little boat tightly as Justin moves it out of the shallows. The calm sea is full of objects that could damage the hull: jagged beams of floating timber, upside-down boats, even a floating car. Angel scans ahead, helping Justin to steer through safely. The further they get from land, the less they have to avoid until finally he is able to accelerate into the open water. She has to admit they make a good team.

The black seabird is still tracking them high up in the blue sky. Angel has to squint into the sun to see it, but even when she can't quite spot the sweep of its wings, she knows it's there, keeping an eye on them.

It's so liberating to be out here on the open sea, away from the grim sights and sickly, cloying smells of Tacloban. As they pull away from the shore the damage becomes less visible. Angel takes a deep breath and fills her lungs with salty sea air. She can almost pretend everything is normal when she glances back at the distant city, although the skyline is strangely uneven and jagged.

She turns towards Samar, bracing herself for how bad it might be.

'Where do your grandparents live?' asks Justin.

'Their farm is a few kilometres inland from Basey,' she replies.

'Inland. That's good, isn't it?'

'I hope so.' Angel goes on to describe her grandparents' farm. It's just about her favourite place in the world. She has spent many happy childhood days there, playing with the baby ducks and the farm dog, Bantay, since he was a little puppy. Best of all is when her grandfather takes them for a ride in the cart with the sweet-natured pony, Blackie, clopping along the dusty roads.

They're much closer now and Justin guides the boat towards the picturesque little beaches and coves that are favourite locations for holiday postcards.

They're still a couple of hundred metres from shore when Justin turns the boat and steers it along the beach. They are both stunned into silence as they contemplate the scale of the damage. Once idyllic white sandy beaches are now entirely buried beneath rubbish. The graceful palm trees that fringed the shoreline are nothing but ragged stumps. Historic beachfront villas that faced Tacloban City, their Spanish architecture giving them a quaint, European charm, are gone forever. The smell of death is here too, and Angel half-closes her eyes to avoid seeing the bodies she knows are there, on the shore and in the shallows. People on the beach wave to them frantically with odd pieces of clothing or torn sheets as flags. This is not a friendly greeting; it's a desperate cry for help.

Justin pulls the boat in at the once-pretty coastal village of Santa Rita. He can tell it's the village from the shape of the shoreline, but nothing else is familiar. He ties up the bangka and removes a piece of the starter engine so that it can't be stolen. 'I'm not taking any chances,' he explains as he buttons it up in one of the deep pouches of his cargo pants.

They scramble out of the boat and look around. Several people are picking listlessly through the rubble. A man wearing nothing but torn shorts is hammering broken pieces of timber onto a ruined house.

'Do you have anything you can give us?' he asks the teenagers and they shake their heads apologetically.

'We've had no help or supplies yet,' he tells them. 'Where the hell is the army?'

They feel helpless. There's so much destruction here that the survivors simply don't know where to start.

'This is terrible,' murmurs Angel. 'They've got nothing.'

'What's the situation further inland?' Justin asks the man.

'I don't know, I just don't know,' the man replies. 'The power is still off, the phones are still down. It's impossible to find out what's going on.'

Angel pulls the mobile phone out of her pocket, now

only half charged, and dials Veronica's number. It's still not responding. She's really starting to get scared now. Samar was on the frontline and obviously took the full force of the storm. It seems like everything was mashed to a pulp here and she's starting to think that it's a miracle anyone survived at all.

Angel's strength is draining fast and her whole body begins to droop. She can feel Justin looking at her worriedly.

'Let's see if we can find some transport,' he says, brightly. 'If they're anywhere, they'll be at the farm.'

They clamber over the debris on the beach and into the village square. Most of the houses are damaged but it's marginally better the further they get from the sea. Angel feels a prickle of hope. If her family were up on the hill, perhaps they're safe?

A group of volunteers has arrived from Cebu only minutes before. They are setting up trestle tables piled with medicines and dressings, and unpacking syringes for vaccinations. Another group has begun handing out bottled water and bags of rice.

'See? Help is slowly coming,' Justin says confidently. He approaches one of the volunteers – a young man with an eager smile – and asks how he got here.

'We managed to get a lift on a truck full of journalists. One of those big vehicles that are high off the ground with big fat tyres. They just crunch over the top of everything!'

'What are the roads like?' Justin enquires.

'They're only partly open and there's still a lot of

flooding. We saw a couple of horses pulling carts – they seemed to get through – but that's about it.'

Angel pipes up, 'Horse and cart! My grandpa and grandma have one of those, they use it for everything.'

'So much for modern transport,' says Justin.

'Times like these we have to fall back on the old ways to survive,' says the volunteer.

'Is the truck still here?' asks Angel.

'Might be,' answers the volunteer. He points to a giant pile of rubble that was once a school building. 'They dropped us behind there about ten minutes ago.'

Justin and Angel move as fast as they can over the scarred terrain and are rewarded by the sight of the tall boxy truck parked behind the school. Several foreign reporters and camera crews are clustered nearby, stretching their legs before they have to climb aboard for the next stage of their bumpy ride.

'Hello? Excuse me, can you help us?' calls out Angel and their pale, unfamiliar faces turn towards her. Suddenly she is paralysed with shyness. Since when did she have the nerve to approach complete strangers – international journalists, no less – and ask them to help her? Before the typhoon she would have died before putting herself forward like this, but now she doesn't hesitate.

'I'm trying to find my mother and brothers. They were sheltering at my grandparents' farm near Basey.'

A slim man with a camera slung over his shoulder and a head as bald and shiny as an egg steps forward and regards them with curiosity.

'Hi, I'm Michael,' he says in a broad American accent, shaking first Justin and then Angel by the hand. 'Where do you need to go? Basey, was it?'

'Anywhere near there would be fine...'

The reporter regards them for a moment.

'Look, we're pretty full with people and camera kit and we're all on deadlines...' Seeing Angel's face fall he stops and sighs. 'Of course. Basey's our next stop. We can fit you in, can't we, guys?'

'Thank you,' beams Angel. 'Thank you so much!'

Everyone climbs into the truck and it slowly moves off. At first, Angel feels quite dizzy; they are so high off the ground and the big tray rocks wildly as they grind over the top of all the rubbish in their path.

'You guys okay?' says a female reporter, hanging on grimly.

'It's like a boat on rough seas!' laughs Justin.

No one says much during the journey. Everyone is transfixed by the view. Not a single roof remains and most of the collapsed buildings are beyond saving. The whole place looks like a giant rubbish tip.

Angel remembers Mrs Fernandez teaching her class about pollution and showing them pictures of the notorious Smokey Mountain rubbish tip in Manila, which stopped operating in the 1990s. Tens of thousands of men, women and children made their homes on and around the tower of landfill, scavenging their livelihoods from other people's waste. Deadly fires were constantly breaking out and many hundreds of the inhabitants perished over the years. Angel was deeply disturbed by the images and she can't help thinking of it now as she watches survivors sifting through the wreckage of Samar.

At one point the truck passes an area where a group of men are digging graves and placing crudely wrapped bodies directly in the ground. Rough pieces of timber have been hammered into crosses to mark where someone is buried. Angel hopes there can be a proper burial later, but for now there is no choice. The stench of death and the risk of disease is too great.

Much of the island of Samar is agricultural land, so while there is less man-made debris as they move through the countryside, field after field of devastated crops stretches out as far as the eye can see. Angel thinks of her grandparents' small acreage. Gloria and Pedro make their main income from growing bananas and taro that they sell at the local market. As far as she can see, not a single banana tree has come through.

Eventually they arrive on the outskirts of the historic town of Basey. In the distance, Angel is glad to see the stone tower of the St Michael church. It appears that the distinctive red, blue and cream structure is intact, though the metal cross on top is bent sideways. She has attended Mass there with her grandparents many times; wedged between them she felt so safe and always loved it when Gloria leaned down and whispered in her ear, 'If these walls could talk, eh?'

A few times the truck is forced to stop and they all jump out to help clear a way through. A woman and two teenage girls are outside a ruined house making a pile of things they want to salvage. The reporters go over and start talking to them. A middle-aged man walking with the aid of a stick limps over to join them.

'Can you tell me what happened here?' the female journalist asks.

The man shakes his head and sighs wearily.

'It was the ocean surge,' he says. 'The wind and rain were very strong. My wife and daughters evacuated to the church up the hill, but I stayed to look after the house. It was frightening but I thought the house would stand up. First, the roof blew off and everything inside was soaked. Then the water came. It was a huge wave, first one, then another and another.'

'How high was it?' asks the reporter, scribbling notes with one hand and holding a long microphone in the other while a cameraman films the exchange.

'Much higher than the house, higher than a tall building. It came in so hard and powerful. It swallowed everything.'

He motions to his injured leg, the calf wrapped in a bloody bandage. 'I was in the downstairs room, sheltering from the rain, then the water came and washed me out, through the roof and over the top of all of those buildings over there.' He motions up the hill. 'Then the wave started to suck me back out again but I grabbed hold of a metal drainpipe. I climbed up onto the roof of a building while the water crashed around me, and clung on through wave after wave. Somehow, during all of that I cut my leg open.'

'You're very lucky you survived,' the reporter says softly.

'We have lost everything, but my wife and daughters and I are alive so yes, we are lucky. Many Basaynons were not.'

Angel feels a chill of dread.

Not much further and the truck is forced to stop for good.

'Looks like this is the end of the line,' announces Michael. 'Is this okay for you guys?'

Justin looks at Angel questioningly and she says, 'This is fine. I know where the farm is from here. It's only a couple of kilometres away. Thanks for the lift!'

As they climb down from the truck Justin spots what looks like an aid staging point up ahead. 'I'll just go and grab some bottles of water and see if they've got anything to eat. You rest here and I'll be back in a few minutes.'

Angel nods gratefully. Her wounded foot is starting to ache again so she walks the short distance to the waterfront and sits down on the edge. It reminds her of the seawall out the front of her home in Tacloban. She looks over at the shoreline of Leyte stretching before her. It's odd to see the flat, clear San Juanico Strait without dozens of fishing boats and pleasure crafts. Usually it's such a busy stretch of water. She smiles, remembering how her mother jokingly refers to it as 'your father's office'. It strikes her that she feels differently about it now. The ocean was always a place of beauty and calm to her, but she's questioning if it's safe anymore, to live so close to the sea. Perhaps Juan will feel the same after all that they've suffered.

Her fingers close around the phone in her pocket, but she doesn't pull it out. The system is probably still down, but now that she's so close to the farm, she'd prefer to find out the fate of her family in person and not at the end of a phone line.

Justin returns soon after with four bottles of water and a small bag of rice.

'We can cook it when we get to the farm,' he says encouragingly.

Using the church tower to get her bearings, Angel leads them in the direction of her grandparents' place. As they move inland away from the town the rubbish is less dense and it doesn't take long for her to come upon the tarred roadway. After a few minutes they hear the clip-clop of a horse and cart behind them.

'Can I give you youngsters a ride?' asks the old man holding the reins. For a split second she thinks it might be Pedro, but this man is much older and even skinnier than her grandfather.

'I live on the other side of Basey, but my son Antonio lives along this road and I haven't heard a word from him since the storm. I've given up waiting for him to answer the phone so I thought I'd come over here myself!' The man speaks lightly, but the teenagers can see the strain in his face.

Something occurs to Angel. 'I think I have met your son. Does he live down the road from my grandparents, Pedro and Gloria?'

'Ah yes, I know those two!' says the man, eagerly. 'Tell me, what have you heard about their fate?'

'Same as you: nothing. The phones are still out,' replies Angel.

'But they say the further inland they were, the better their chances,' adds Justin.

'That's true,' the old man nods. 'My place was damaged but we all came through in one piece and that's the main thing.'

Justin and Angel climb into the back of the old wooden cart and sit on the floor. The old man wants to talk but he's kept busy navigating his pony around obstacles and flooded areas on the road. When they begin to head up the hill the man's sharp eyes bring good news.

'Can you see how the damage changes? It's the same at my place. The wind smashed everything up, but it doesn't look like the seawater reached this far.'

'That's what caused the most destruction,' says Justin.

'You know, I don't think that most of us really understood what a "surge" was. If they had called it a wall of water like a tidal wave or a tsunami, a lot more people would have got out,' the man says.

'You're right,' says Justin. 'The warnings weren't clear enough.'

Angel's heart has been pounding the closer they get to the farm and as they approach the gate to her grandparents' property she feels like it's going to jump right out of her mouth.

'We can walk from here, it's not far,' she tells the old man as he slows the pony to a stop.

'Salamat, mano. Thank you, sir,' says Justin as they jump down from the cart.

'Good luck to you, children,' he says.

'Say hello to Antonio for us,' says Justin encouragingly, and the old man salutes them with a wave as he heads off down the road.

'Basta ang Waray, hindi uurong sa away!' he calls after them.

Angel smiles weakly at the old saying about Waray people never backing down from a fight, but in truth she feels scared stiff at the prospect of what she might find now that they've reached their destination.

Fifteen

Angel fights to steady her breathing as she stands with one hand on her grandparents' gate. It is suddenly hard to move.

'It's going to be alright, you'll see,' Justin says calmly. 'Let's go.' He links his arm through hers and they begin to walk up the driveway.

Around a slight bend the house is revealed – it's still standing. Angel lets out a whimper and begins to move faster. The front door bursts open and two small figures run out into the front yard, shrieking with laughter as they chase after a ball.

'It's the boys,' says Angel and she breaks into a limping run.

'CRISTIAN! CARLO!' she shouts.

The figures stop and turn towards her.

'ANGEL!' they both yell at the same time. 'Mama! It's Angel. SHE'S HERE!'

Cristian reaches her first and he nearly knocks her over with the force of his hug. 'Mama said you would be

okay, but I thought you … when you didn't come, I …'
and he bursts into loud sobs.

Carlo bowls into her next. 'I knew it, I knew it, I knew
it!' he bellows gleefully.

Angel looks up and there's her mother standing on
the front porch with her hands clapped over her mouth,
shaking her head in disbelief. And then around the side
of the house her grandfather and grandmother appear,
whooping with joy and hurrying towards her as fast as
their old legs will carry them.

Angel will never forget this moment.

The only thing marring the reunion is Juan's absence.
While the others are rejoicing, Carlo scampers up to
Justin.

'Where's Papa? Did you bring Papa?' He grabs
Justin's arm and begins dragging him back up the driveway. 'Did you leave him back here?'

Angel quickly explains that Juan is alive and recovering in the hospital, and that he is going to be alright too.
That's when Veronica, overcome with emotion, dissolves
into tears and falls to her knees. Angel understands her
mother's reaction. Her whole family has survived. It's
nothing short of a miracle.

Gloria can't stop fussing, dusting, wiping and tidying
the little house as best she can. She has a permanent
grin and she keeps dabbing at her eyes with the old towel
tucked into her waistband. Every time she goes past
Justin, she grasps him by the hands and says something

like, 'Salamat, idoy, young man. Thank you so much for bringing her back to us.' At first he responded with, 'Angel was determined to get here!' and then, 'It was a team effort!' but now he just nods and grins, pleased to have played his part in this happy reunion.

Since she arrived, Angel has been telling them everything that's happened since her mother and brothers left Tacloban six days before. When she gets to the part about Mrs Reyes rescuing her and then the two of them clinging to the power pole, her audience is thunderstruck.

'Little old Mrs Reyes? I don't believe you!' says Cristian.

'I do,' says Pedro. 'She is a very tough woman.'

'Was,' whispers Angel.

'What do you mean?' asks Veronica.

Angel falters. 'She made it through the storm, but afterwards … it was all too much for her.'

She tells them about her journey with Mrs Reyes, and how they ended up at Issy's house, where Mrs Reyes spent her final days.

'It was her heart. She'd been through so much …'

Wiping her eyes, Veronica says, 'I'm so glad that she was with Danilo and Maria. They would have looked after her the best they could.'

'Mrs Reyes saved Angel,' says Cristian.

'She's a hero,' adds Carlo.

'God bless her,' says Gloria with a sad smile.

Angel continues her story and the mood lightens when she describes how she found Juan in the airport hospital.

'Papa's head was wrapped in bandages, but I recognised his hair.'

'Aha! The famous white streak!' says Pedro, and they all laugh.

She recounts what Juan had told her of his ordeal and how he'd ended up there.

'What did Papa look like?' asks Cristian.

Angel remembers the frail figure in the hospital bed. 'Very tired and sore,' she responds. 'But they say he will heal as good as new.'

Gloria claps her hands sharply. 'Pangaon kita! You must be starving!' Pedro goes outside to salvage some of the bananas from the ruined crop while Gloria makes a fire to cook some of the rice Justin brought.

The electricity and phones are still off, but the farmhouse gets its water from tanks and although one was knocked off its stand and leaked its load, the other is intact. Gloria has stockpiled a few days' worth of food. She puts some tea from a jar in a teapot and pumps some water from the tank into a bucket, using it to fill a blackened old kettle. When the fire is going she lets it burn down a little and then puts the kettle on to boil. A few minutes later she is pouring strong black tea into seven chipped mugs.

When the rice is ready they all sit around on upturned buckets and crates and eat a simple meal. Justin and Angel do a brief rundown of how they fixed the bangka and motored across the strait this morning.

'You came on your own?' frowns Veronica.

'Justin is a great boatman,' says Angel quickly. 'We were perfectly safe.'

'I've been out many times with my father,' explains Justin. 'We went very slowly and Angel did the navigating.'

Gloria takes the plates and gives them to the twins, who reluctantly carry them out to be washed at the big plastic tub near the pump. When they have gone she asks softly: 'Have many died?'

'Thousands,' answers Justin bluntly.

Angel continues quietly. 'For the first few days there were bodies lying around everywhere. I tried not to look at them, but it was unavoidable. There was nothing to wrap them in, nowhere to put them.'

'No dignity at all,' says Veronica, horrified.

'Now most of them have been collected and taken away by hygiene crews,' says Justin. 'But here in Samar today we saw people burying bodies directly in the earth.'

The adults shake their heads sadly. Angel can see that while they are not surprised to hear of the great loss of life, it's still hard for them to comprehend the scale of the disaster. They've been relatively lucky here at the farm. There are trees down and roofs off the outbuildings but the house has only minor damage. The worst of it for Pedro and Gloria is that they lost their two cows and the banana crop has been flattened. The old couple will have to live off their taro crop alone for some time to come.

The boys come back inside. 'Tell us what happened here,' says Angel, eager to change the subject. 'How did you get through it with so little damage?'

'You know your grandpa,' smiles Veronica. 'Every year he thinks up new strategies to protect the house from storms.'

Pedro explains how he took a set of strong coloured ropes and slung them through the eaves and anchored the ends to steel bolts in the cement floor, tying down the roof. The ropes strained and twanged as the wind swirled under the eaves, but they held fast. He was worried about the animals in the outbuildings though, and in the middle of it all he left the house to check on them.

'Grandpa didn't come back for ages,' Carlo says, trembling at the memory.

'It was only about ten minutes,' says Pedro.

'He was so brave,' says Cristian.

'I've seen a lot of typhoons,' the old man laughs, 'and I'm damned if I'll let them get the better of me. Even the mighty Yolanda!'

'Mama was brave too,' says Carlo.

'I nearly drowned before I got here!' Veronica says.

Gloria clucks and waves a finger at her daughter.

Angel is surprised. 'I thought you all made it to the farm before the storm hit?' she says to her mother.

'Yes, but that's not the whole story,' admits Veronica. 'I did a really stupid thing on the way. I should have known better.'

'Tell them, Mama,' begs Carlo.

Veronica begins. 'It started on Samar when we couldn't get a lift. Every vehicle was full of people rushing to escape the storm so we had to walk. The boys were wet and tired and I was so worried that we would get caught out in the open. Every time we passed a sign pointing to a coastal village I was tempted to seek shelter…'

'Thank goodness you didn't!' says Angel. 'The beach was the worst place to be.'

'I know that now. It was only the thought of Grandma and Grandpa worrying about us that kept me going. And then we had a stroke of luck. Their neighbour, Antonio, went past us on his motorbike. He had offered to look for us on the road because he knew there would be no transport.'

'His father was the one who gave me and Justin a lift here!' says Angel.

'Is he okay?' asks Justin.

'Yes, he walked over after the storm to check on us,' says Veronica.

'They are a good family. Very caring,' says Gloria.

'Anyway,' continues Veronica, 'he wasn't able to carry all three of us plus our bags on his bike. He said he would take the boys to the farm first and then come back for me. I was so relieved when they set off, but hours later when he hadn't come back I panicked and started walking.

'When I reached the low part of the road I realised why Antonio hadn't come back – the road was flooded. I was so scared that in my mind I had no choice but to keep going. I put the bag with the water containers on one shoulder and the other bag with the food on top of my head, steadying it with my hand until I felt balanced. Then I stepped into the water, keeping to the centre of the road so I wouldn't get sucked into a drain.'

'Oh, Mama.' Angel shakes her head.

'I know, I know. Madness! At first it wasn't too deep,

but then it was up to my ankles and then my knees. And then – ugh! – something slid past my leg and I realised it was a snake caught up in the floodwater. It was all I could do not to scream my head off.' She takes a deep breath. 'Of course I fell. I let go of the bags but there was nothing to hang on to, nothing to stop me being swept away.'

She pauses for a moment and smiles. 'Do you know, all I could think about as I struggled in the water was your grandma telling me over and over again when I was growing up that I must *never* try to walk through a flash flood, especially on that part of the road where the hill curves steeply towards the sea.'

Gloria laughs and Angel joins in. 'And I don't know how many times you have told us exactly the same thing!'

'I was terrified, but through the wind I heard someone calling: "Veronica! Veronica! SWIM!" So I turned over onto my belly and kicked towards the voice until someone grabbed me and dragged me up out of the water. It was Antonio and he shouted at me: "Don't you remember your mother telling you never to cross a flash flood?" I think he was more scared than I was.'

Angel shakes her head with relief. It seems that many of them survived Yolanda by the skin of their teeth. Even after Antonio dropped Veronica at the farm and they were all inside safely together, the ordeal was not over.

'When your grandfather went out to check on the animals we were very worried,' Gloria confirms.

'Then the door flew open with a crash and he burst in yelling: "Get the animals inside. The roofs are off the sheds. They won't survive."'

Veronica had followed her father back out into the night, leaving the boys and their grandmother wild-eyed with fear. The cows had already escaped the shed and taken off into the rain but Blackie was still tied up and panicky as the last sheet of roof iron swung crazily like a kite. Veronica had grabbed the pony by the halter and frantically fumbled with the rope, trying to untie it with her wet hands.

She saw Pedro emerge from the other shed with a chicken under each arm and two in each hand. 'I have to get the ducks and their babies,' he had yelled at her, hurtling towards the house. 'Quick, bring Blackie inside!'

Gloria was waiting in the house with an open cardboard box. 'Grandpa dumped the six chickens inside and rushed out again to collect the ducks,' she said. 'Only when your mother and grandfather and the pony and the ducks were all safely inside the house did we barricade the door again with chairs.'

'You should have seen the boys,' chuckles Veronica. 'They were delighted with their indoor zoo! Blackie was standing in the middle of the room watching the ducks and the chickens were scampering free across the floor. The dog was so confused. It was crazy!'

'We found some knobbly old carrots and fed them to Blackie,' says Carlo.

Veronica chimes in, laughing. 'She was so happy

nodding her head up and down and spitting bits of carrot all over the floor!'

'I must admit, it was funny, or it is in hindsight at least,' Pedro says ruefully.

And that was how it had gone for several hours. The wind howled and the roof sprang numerous leaks but it stayed on. The boys dozed intermittently and the animals settled in and seemed content to wait it out. They were all wide awake, though, when the storm reached its peak. Veronica and her father anchored the ropes with their own weight while Gloria crouched in a corner with the boys and the old dog, Bantay.

Finally the whistling wind began to ease. Their ears were ringing from hours of blasting rain pounding on the iron roof. Gloria picked up a mop and began cleaning up the water on the floor. Pedro peeled open the cardboard from one of the windows and peeked outside. In the dim morning light he saw sheets of iron strewn around the banana patch. All of the plants were bent double. The outbuildings had lost their roofs and doors, several large trees were down and away in the distance were two still, dark shapes lying on the ground, which he guessed were the cows.

They moved the furniture and opened the door. One by one, Pedro unwound the ropes and pulled them through and out of the eaves. They'd done their job and saved the roof. Slowly and deliberately, he coiled each rope neatly, tied them off and put them in a colourful pile next to the front door for next time.

'I went for a walk over the farm,' says Pedro, sipping

his tea thoughtfully. 'I pulled a tiny green banana off a dead plant, and I knew there would be no fruit to sell this year. Then I stood still and looked around me: from the flattened plants to the damaged sheds to the house still standing. I saw my old pony grazing happily with ducks and chickens at her feet, and my two grandsons running around to burn off some energy. And I knew in that moment that I must give thanks because it could have been much, much worse.'

Gloria pats her husband on the shoulder and says softly, 'Padayon an kinabuhi. Life goes on.'

Sixteen

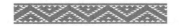

As soon as it's light, the whole family climbs into the old cart. It's a tight squeeze but most of the journey is downhill and Justin and the boys jump off and walk a large part of the way. It takes the pony an hour or so to pull them down to the place where Juan's bangka is still anchored. Cristian and Carlo are particularly shocked to see what remains of the pretty seaside village where they come to play when they visit their grandparents.

'No more sandcastles,' says Carlo.

'One day it will be cleared,' says Pedro soothingly. 'The trees will recover and it will be our beautiful little beach once again.'

Pedro and Gloria are staying on Samar to begin the many repairs on their property. The others are going to take the boat back to Tacloban.

'Will Papa be waiting for us?' asks Carlo.

'I'm not sure,' says Angel. 'He might still be at the hospital.'

'If he is, we'll go and visit,' says Veronica firmly.

Angel gives her grandparents Father Jose's old mobile

phone and charger. 'Once the phones are working again on Samar, we'll ring you and let you know what has happened. We need to stay in touch!'

Veronica's phone is still almost fully charged and she turns it on now to see if there is any mobile reception yet. Nothing.

The children hug their grandparents. Pedro shakes Justin's hand. 'Come back and see us, Justin. You're welcome any time, idoy.'

'Now make sure they all get back safely!' says Gloria, pulling him into an awkward hug. Blushing fiercely, Justin scurries into the boat and fixes the part back into the starter motor. The others climb in and position themselves evenly along the narrow vessel. It's unusual for it to carry so many people but the little boat is well balanced and holds steady in the water with barely a wobble. Justin starts the engine after a couple of tries and they pull away towards Leyte.

Angel, Carlo and Cristian turn their faces into the wind as Justin guns it towards Tacloban City. Carlo starts singing his favourite Jireh Lim song. Angel twists around and gives her mother an encouraging smile. *Wherever you are ...* She knows that Veronica won't be able to relax until they are all together again.

When they are near the shore Justin slows the boat and drives it along parallel to the seawall so that Veronica and the boys can see what the city looks like now. Despite the cleaning up that's been done there's still a lot of debris in the water. More than once Justin has to slow right down and steer around large obstructions like a car wedged by rocks and sand, or a boat embedded prow-down in the seabed. Carlo has stopped singing and both he and his brother are unusually still as they witness the scale of the destruction for the first time.

'Look!' Cristian indicates a big sign floating in the water: 'Delicious Fried Chicken!' it reads.

'And there!' Carlo points at a small pink bicycle drifting by. He raises his eyes to what's left of the city.

'It doesn't look like home,' he says.

'It looks like a movie,' says Cristian with a frown. 'A disaster movie.'

They pass the town hall, high on the hill, then the Santo Niño church, and Veronica exclaims with relief to see that it's mostly intact.

It's the simple houses that people lived in and the shops that people used every day that have been annihilated by Yolanda's fury, thinks Angel. And it's the ordinary people who will suffer most in the days to come. She wonders how long it will take for life to get back to normal in this town where she has lived her whole life.

Justin pulls the little boat up near their house. He ties it to a bollard, and they all climb up over the cement seawall. The boys can scarcely believe their eyes. A big fishing boat is sitting on the top of a mountain of debris right in the middle of their neighbourhood. Dozens of people are swarming over the piles of timber and cement like ants. The air is filled with the sound of hammering and sawing.

Angel takes Veronica's hand. Behind them, the twins meekly walk either side of Justin. Slowly the little group makes its way towards the house. They pass the site of Mrs Reyes's home, now just a bare patch of cement. Veronica bends down to the little pile of things that Mrs Reyes pulled out of the rubble when she and Angel first returned after the storm. She picks up a broken piece of ceramic plate with a pretty pink flower etched on it and tucks it in her pocket along with a smudged photograph showing a young Mrs Reyes, smiling as she holds her baby up to the camera.

As they approach their home, Veronica is gripping Angel's hand so hard that it hurts. *Will he be here?* Angel wonders. She can see that the area around the building is a little less cluttered than when she left, as if someone has been clearing rubbish away. But anyone could do that, she reasons…

And then in one glorious moment the speculating is over. For there, standing in the doorway of their house, is Juan. He looks thin and drawn but his face is lit with a smile of pure joy. One of his arms is in a sling and he's holding something up in the other one, waving it at them. Suddenly, the phone in Veronica's pocket starts to beep loudly and Juan shouts: 'It's ringing! Finally, it's ringing!'

Everyone starts laughing as they come together: Veronica and the twins embracing Juan, Angel stepping in for a quick hug, too, and Justin standing by, once again a happy witness.

'When did the hospital discharge you?' asks Angel.

'They let me go this morning. I came straight here.'

'Are you alright though?' asks his wife with concern, carefully stroking his bandaged head.

'My arm will take a few weeks to heal but they tell me my head will be as good as new in a few days. They lent me this old phone to check in now that the system is up again.'

'Justin drove your bangka, Papa,' says Cristian excitedly.

'He helped me get to Samar, Papa,' explains Angel. 'He helped me find Mama and the boys, just as you wanted me to.'

'You took *my boat*?' Juan scoffs in mock horror. 'I hope you looked after it!'

'I did my best, mano,' stutters Justin nervously.

'He even found a new engine and installed it himself!' adds Angel.

'I am in your debt, Justin,' says Juan gravely. 'I don't know how I can ever repay you for helping to return my family to me.'

Angel is taken aback by Justin's response. 'It was mostly Angel. She's pretty resourceful,' he says solemnly. 'And also very brave. I was just happy to help.'

'Thank you, Justin,' says Veronica.

'Now I should get back to my family,' says Justin. 'You are all welcome to stay with us, if you wish. We don't have much, but we do have a roof over our heads.'

'God bless you,' says Veronica.

Juan shakes the young man's hand.

'Please give my love to Issy and your mother and father,' says Angel. 'I hope to see them very soon.'

'We have some good stories to tell them, don't we?' smiles Justin.

'Only if you stop calling me pipsqueak,' Angel smiles back.

After Justin has gone, the family wanders around the site of their former home. The boys scurry about rescuing familiar bits and pieces: a broken scooter, a three-legged stool, their old trumpo. Miraculously, the wooden top spins as smoothly as ever!

Juan and Veronica slowly circle the damaged building, holding hands and quietly exchanging their stories as they assess the extent of the structural damage. Eventually Veronica ducks inside, kicking at the mud-smeared household items that are strewn all over the floor. 'Not much worth saving here,' she sighs.

Angel pokes her head through the door. She has mixed feelings about her home now. After all, this is where she spent the most terrifying night of her life. Her eyes slide upwards and she shudders, remembering how she nearly drowned, trapped beneath the roof. Veronica puts her arm around Angel and gives her a squeeze as she surveys the wreckage.

Bending down she retrieves a navy blue shoe that she always used to wear to church. Spying the other one she vigorously scrapes the mud off them both and guides them onto her feet, but the leather has shrunk and they are too small for her now. She shrugs and puts them aside.

'We have been incredibly lucky, you and I,' she tells Angel. 'We must never forget that.'

'Mama! Papa! Look what we found!' The boys are shrieking excitedly.

Veronica and Angel step outside and there are Cristian and Carlo, each grasping an end of the old taklub.

'It was caught underneath a piece of the seawall!' shouts Cristian.

'It's not even broken!' crows Carlo.

The boys pass it reverently to their father. He sits down and starts to run his good hand over the familiar bamboo sticks of the basket. 'I thought it had gone forever,' he says softly. 'My lucky charm.'

Angel sits down next to him and, after a while, plucks up the courage to ask: 'Papa, will you rebuild the house?'

'I'm not sure, Angel,' he replies. 'It's a big job. What do you think?'

'Well,' she says slowly, 'I can't help thinking what if we rebuild here and another big storm comes? I mean, could this happen again?'

Her mother and father have been asking themselves the same question.

'We have a lot to talk about,' Juan says firmly. He stands up and secures the taklub to a sturdy pylon. 'For now, we must find a place to sleep tonight. Come on everyone, we'll come back tomorrow.'

The five of them walk up onto the main road. The debris is piled high on either side, but the rutted bitumen is now clear. Juan flags down a passing truck heading to the city and they all jump into the back. Angel points out the long queues for rice and medicine as they pass and the lines winding down the street from the mobile water-treatment vans. Children wave merrily at them from the shelters.

'I stayed in one just like that the other night,' Angel tells her mother. 'It was clean and safe.' Veronica nods approvingly at the brightly coloured washing hanging in the windows.

Everywhere they look, people are clearing and sweeping, fixing and building. It may not look like much now, but there is a dogged sense of determination among the Taclobanons.

The truck lets them off near Santo Niño and they walk towards the church. Angel notices that since she was last here the streets are looking much better, but nothing's normal yet. She points out the police boat in the middle of the road to her brothers as they pass by.

Veronica examines the outside of the church and the damage to the steeple.

'Not too bad,' she says quietly.

The interior is calm and tranquil – a welcome oasis after the hot, busy streets outside. The damaged pews have been cleared away so the church looks quite empty. There are only a handful of other people present and Father Jose is busy elsewhere. The boys run around, chasing little sparrows, as they have always done. They're happy that at least here inside the church things haven't changed all that much. Veronica and Juan sit together, quietly praying in one of the remaining pews.

Angel makes her way to the back of the church where the lists of missing people are still pinned to the noticeboard. She leafs through the pages until she finds the names of her mother and brothers. Grasping the pen on a string she puts a line through their names and next to each one, she writes: 'Found safe and well.'

It's over.

Seventeen

Angel stands up and dusts off her knees. She picks a few bits of dried grass off her skirt, and gazes out at the flat, glassy ocean. It's so peaceful up here on the hill with the breeze rustling through the spindly trees. A good spot for a grave.

She takes a piece of rag out of her pocket and runs it over the headstone.

It's that time of year again and heavy clouds are threatening rain, but she cleans it anyway, scrubbing the dust out of the engraving and off the varnished stone.

Mrs Reyes would have liked it here, Angel is sure of that. Of course, she would have preferred to be down close to the seashore where she lived most of her life, but after everything that's happened Angel is happier to see her old friend laid to rest on high ground. It's much the same view anyway; out over the city, down to the church and across the water.

She rakes the last of the leaves away from the grave, smoothing out the loose dirt, and gives the inscription a final polish:

Luisa C. Reyes
A strong and brave woman.
Lost to us after Yolanda.
Much missed.

'I'll come back soon,' she whispers.

Angel makes her way down the hill and places the rake at the back door of a little cement house. She shakes off her sandals and steps inside, the soles of her feet padding silently across the cool floor.

Their own house, so close to the water, is gone. One day they all stood and watched as Juan's legacy was bulldozed. According to the government it was too close to the water and residents were advised to move away from the flat land near the sea. Juan didn't need much persuading; he didn't want his family living in the path of another storm like Yolanda. He accepted a parcel of land further up the hill, and began to rebuild. In the mornings he went out fishing and in the afternoons, while Veronica dried fish for the market, he built them a new house.

Angel and the boys helped as best they could. They salvaged tin from the ruins around them and pulled a water tank from the rubble. An unbroken window, a few roof beams, an old kitchen sink were all recycled from the remnants of abandoned buildings. Juan snapped the front door from their old house off its hinges, repainted it vivid blue and fixed it at the front of their new house on the hill overlooking the sea. They rescued pots and pans and bits of cutlery but there wasn't much more than that left at the old place. Now their new home is all but finished.

It's a simple home, much like the one the family lived in before the storm, with one large room downstairs and a ladder up to a sleeping platform. The kitchen is in one corner and there's a side door out to a little washroom. Juan has built a covered porch at the front, too, with a panoramic view over the city and the sea.

It's still early but the living area and the banigs on the platform are empty so Angel pokes her head out onto the porch, where Juan, Veronica and the boys are eating a breakfast of rice and boiled bananas. Juan is sipping his usual sweet cup of coffee.

'Pangaon kita,' says her mother. 'Come and eat before these three gobble it all up!' It's one year today since the super storm struck. One year since their lives were changed forever. Angel meets her mother's eyes. She knows what she's thinking. So much has happened in a year.

The streets of Tacloban are mostly clear. The mountains of rubble along the seashore have been bulldozed into piles and lifted into great trucks and then tipped into landfill. Boats have been towed back out to sea, except the biggest, heaviest ones. Stuck fast, they remain where the flood left them, huge urban memorials to the storm and its victims. Cars and motorbikes have come down from trees. Damaged houses have been repaired or demolished. Shops have been fixed. Markets have reopened.

They're among the lucky ones. Recovery has been very slow and some people are still living in tents a full year after the storm. Angel knows it's because of Juan's building skills and self-reliance that they have a roof over their heads. She's grateful.

The children have been back at school for several months. Some of their classmates are still missing and there will be memorial services for them this week. But today the family is heading into the city to celebrate Angel's recent birthday and to mark the anniversary of Yolanda.

After breakfast, Angel puts on a long, soft, green dress that her mother has made specially for her birthday. It has tiny flowers embroidered across the bodice in yellow and pink. Veronica spent many evenings doing the intricate needlework while the children slept. They had so many expenses after the typhoon that they could not afford nice things, but Veronica was determined her daughter would have something special to wear when she turned fourteen.

Angel brushes her long dark hair in smooth, even strokes. These days she lets it flow freely across her shoulders and down her back. The pearl her father gave her glows warmly against the soft skin of her throat. Out of habit she rolls it between her fingers, enjoying its smooth silkiness. She keeps it on all the time now. Since the storm she's gone to sleep every night with her hand clasped around it protectively. Angel believes it helps to soothe bad memories and keep nightmares at bay.

Juan is waiting on the front porch and Angel joins him. He is shading his eyes with his hand, watching the big black seabird circle slowly above the house, its wings at full stretch. Angel hasn't seen it for some months now, but she is glad to see it back today of all days. She remembers how she used to believe that it was a bad omen. Now she thinks of it as a strong, resilient survivor – a true Taclobanon!

She puts a hand up and waves at it. She could almost swear that the bird dips a wing at her as it turns and flies towards the strait.

'Our friend, hey?' Juan says to Angel. 'He's always hanging around.'

The rest of the family gathers on the front porch in their best clothes and together they walk down the hill. Many of their neighbours are among those still living in tents and half-repaired houses, their roofs swathed in sheets of bright plastic. But the roads are all clear and the power is on.

While her family goes on ahead, Angel ducks into Barangay 18, past the faded sign reading 'WE NEED FOOD', which is still nailed to a power pole on the corner. At Issy's home all the mud and mess is gone and the yard is swept clean. There are chickens pecking at some loose grain and a dog is asleep on the path. The toppled water tank is upright again and the broken porch post has been repaired. The little house has had a fresh coat of white paint and there are shiny new sheets of iron on the roof.

'Issy!' Angel calls out. 'It's me, Angel. Are you ready?'

Issy appears at the front door wearing a bright, pretty dress covered in pink and orange swirls. Her dark hair is piled high in a bun and two perfect corkscrew curls frame her smiling face.

'You look gorgeous!' She admires Angel's new dress. 'I love that colour! Hey, I forgot to give you this.' She presses a small envelope into her friend's hand. Inside is a photo that was taken of the two of them last year on Angel's birthday. They're both smiling into the camera, arms around each other, oblivious to the fact that they are days away from disaster.

'Ayo, come on, kuya, we're going!' Issy calls into the house. 'He's probably fussing with his new "style",' she grins.

Sure enough, Justin emerges from the house smoothing down his neat ponytail. He has much longer hair now, which he wears loosely pulled back and his strong, high cheekbones and large, dark eyes are much more noticeable.

'Many happy returns for Wednesday,' he says to Angel.

'Thanks,' says Angel, flattered that he remembered.

There is an easy friendship between them now. They still disagree on many things, but these days they can joke about their differences of opinion. After Yolanda, Justin has a new respect for his little sister's best friend and Angel knows now that underneath his gruff exterior is a thoughtful nature.

The three teenagers walk up to the road and jump into a passing jeepney. Some of the vehicles wrecked in the storm have been fixed and other new ones have been brought in from places like Manila. They disembark when they get near the waterfront. The harbour is clear again, although a few overturned boats remain submerged in the water. They'll probably remain there until the ocean moves them.

Angel turns and looks up at the town hall with the Filipino flag. The broken windows have been repaired and the sweeping lawns out front are lush and green again. There are still a few aid agencies set up there, even a year later. People are still very much in need.

Today is an important milestone for the Santo Niño church. The exterior has been freshly painted white and all of the pews have finally been repaired. Like everything after Yolanda, progress has been slow and the final fixes are still being made inside. In that sense its recovery reflects the long, painful journey back to normality that everyone in Tacloban has experienced.

Father Jose and the nuns have resurrected the gardens, digging over the salty soil, laying down fertiliser and replanting so the area around the church is green and colourful. Two frangipanis that survived Yolanda have burst into flower, one pink, one yellow. A top architect has led the process, but parishioners have helped to repaint the window frames, repair the roof and then carefully replace the precious panes of stained glass.

When the families enter from the back of the church it gleams newly fresh and white, aside from a few remaining ladders and tools. The pews are lined up in rows, the ceiling fans are whirring and the sunlight is spraying rainbows onto the sparkling walls through the coloured windows. A couple of little birds are spinning through the eaves and the boys eye them with interest, but they no longer chase after them. Carlo and Cristian are nine years old now and they are more interested in chasing a soccer ball.

Father Jose is at the front of the church and he peers at them through shiny new glasses, smiling in his gentle way.

'Welcome,' he says to the group. 'I'm so pleased to see you here all together for the big event!'

The church is filling up with people. A woman stands and sings 'Amazing Grace' in a strong, clear voice and several people join in. Candles are lit, tears are shed, and people who haven't seen each other since before Yolanda clasp hands, forever connected by what they've experienced.

Angel sits and listens for a while. Then she stands up and walks to the noticeboard at the back of the church where the list still flaps in the breeze from the fans. She remembers writing her family's names on it, and then the pervasive relief of crossing them off one by one. Many names are crossed off with notes next to them, like 'found in Samar', or 'recovering in the mobile hospital,' or 'evacuated early' or 'found safe and well'. Many names are still uncrossed and this is why the list remains here, as a kind of memorial to those who died in the storm. Sadly, Nadia's father was one of them. He drowned when his jeepney was swept away and Angel's heart aches for her friend, who has moved to Cebu to live with her uncle's family.

At the end of the service Father Jose asks everyone to move outside for a special ceremony. A new sign has been erected at the front.

Father Jose addresses the expectant crowd.

'After a difficult year, I stand here with you, the survivors of the storm. Against great odds you have fought hard in a climate of adversity. You have gone without food and water, you have suffered without shelter, you have lost loved ones. And in the midst of all this, you have picked yourselves up, you have dusted yourselves off and you have rebuilt your lives. I can't tell you how proud I am to be a part of this community.'

People smile and murmur appreciatively.

'As you can see, here at the Santo Niño church we have also been regenerating and rebuilding, and today we unveil our new church sign.'

The priest gives a signal and a sheet that's been covering the sign drops away. Father Jose reads in a loud voice: 'Santa Niño Church, Tacloban City. Proudly Standing Strong.'

The crowd begins to applaud and cheer. Angel claps so hard that her hands hurt and her face aches from smiling. It may only be a building, but this church means so much to the many members of the congregation who faced down Yolanda.

Soon a street band begins to play and an impromptu party starts up. There's dancing and singing and even a small puppet show for the children. Angel joins in with the others, but after a while she wants a break from the festivities. She crosses the road and walks down to the sea, the sound of music and laughter in her ears and the salty air filling her lungs.

Juan keeps his bangka here now, tied up along with the other little fishing boats, bobbing in the water on the rising tide. Someone is already sitting there on the seawall and she realises that it's Justin, taking some time out just like her. He turns his head, and before she can ask, he indicates the spot next to him. She sits down and the two of them stare out at the water in silent companionship.

'You know, a few months after the storm I decided that as soon as I finished school I would leave Tacloban and never come back,' says Justin.

Angel is surprised, but she also understands. The process of recovery has been slow and difficult.

He continues: 'I felt there was no future for me here. It was no place for a young person to start out on life.'

'And now?' asks Angel.

'This is my home. I will always love it here. What about you?'

Angel thinks for a moment before she replies. 'Maybe I will leave one day – there are things that I want to do and see. But I think that I will always return, no matter what. Yolanda taught me that.'

They stay there silently for several minutes more. Dark, steel-grey clouds are piling up on each other the way they do before a storm. The sea is still flat, but there's the occasional ripple as a gust of wind rises and then falls away.

'There's going to be a storm,' Angel says, shivering, though not from cold.

'Looks like it,' replies Justin.

Angel eyes him thoughtfully. 'Not a super storm though, right?'

He laughs. 'Not today!'

Fat, heavy raindrops begin to fall and the two of them stand and walk back up the hill towards the music and the dancing and the people they love.

Author's note

I landed in Tacloban City about a day after Typhoon Yolanda hit.

Cameraman David Leland and I had flown overnight from our base in Bangkok, where I was the Australian Broadcasting Corporation's South-East Asia correspondent. In the dark hours of the morning we then caught a Philippine Air Force C-130 into the disaster zone.

We were one of the first international TV crews to make our way in. The flight was standing room only, packed with soldiers, relief workers and a four-wheel drive van sitting on a pallet that we all had to push against to stop it sliding backwards down the centre of the plane as we took off into the stormy sky.

We flew into a dim, drizzly morning at the devastated airport, where the roof was in shredded pieces lying around the carpark along with rows of chairs flung from the terminal, which was awash with thick mud.

The scene was truly shocking, with upturned cars everywhere, buildings and trees down, debris and water and mud from the storm surge, and of course the bodies of the dead.

Initially we had no vehicle to leave the airport, which is some distance from the city, so we walked out as far as we could to film the devastation and talk to the shell-shocked people, who were dazed by the trauma of what had happened. We returned to the ruins of the terminal to use our satellite equipment to file the first of our stories. It was still raining and water was pouring through the roof so we dragged some bits of tin under one of the less leaky sections and popped up the two dome tents we had brought with us. That night we slept for an hour or two surrounded by refugees from the storm who had walked to the airport, desperate for a way out of the flattened city. Their numbers would grow in the coming days, with soldiers eventually forcibly holding people back from rushing onto departing planes.

That night cargo aircraft and helicopters landed one after another, spraying mud and grit over all of those waiting in the hope that they could leave.

The next day, with the help of our Filipino producer Sol Vanzi, who helped me check some of the facts in *Angel*, we found a kind businessman with a functioning car who agreed to take us into town and give us a bed for a couple of nights at his largely undamaged house up on the hill behind the city. We would eventually have to leave due to looting and shots fired in the street outside, but it gave us a place to work for a day or two until we had to relocate again.

The scale of the disaster was quickly apparent when we left the airport. The wind and storm surge had virtually flattened Tacloban. Cement buildings had been smashed; powerlines were down; cars, couches, TVs were in trees; boats were sitting on piles of debris nowhere near the ocean. Survivors sat dazed, or rushed to talk to us, to show us their ruined houses or to ask us to tell their families they were okay.

Many told amazing stories of escape, clinging to power or light poles, escaping through ceilings, retreating to higher ground while being chased by the ocean. All told of the loss of family and friends, either confirmed dead or disappeared.

In some parts of the city there was so much debris that it created what felt like tunnels to drive through, the walls higher than the car.

Communication, as always in disasters, was a huge problem, along with lack of power and fuel. The priest at Santo Niño was very proud of his idea to bring in a generator so people could charge their phones, and rightly so. Lack of network, however, remained a problem and people constantly asked me if they could use our satellite phone to call their families. I started taking email addresses and phone numbers to let people know that their loved ones were safe.

The characters in this book are fictional, of course, but the description and narrative reflects what I saw when covering Typhoon Yolanda in the Philippines.

The list of names of the missing and dead at the back of the church, for example, is one of my enduring memories of the assignment.

As always in challenging situations, the strength of the human spirit displayed was inspiring, particularly in communities already challenged by things like poverty and lack of support to deal with disasters.

The situation after Yolanda was frustrating because aid was slow to flow. That's always the way as authorities mobilise and then sort out who's in charge and how to deploy help, but the self-reliance and optimism of the Filipinos was a privilege to witness and report.

I have not yet returned to Tacloban City. I hope to one day, but it's a place I will never forget.

Timeline

2013 2 November A low-pressure system develops 425 km east-south-east of Pohnpei in the Pacific islands of Micronesia.

4 November The system intensifies and heads west towards Palau. The Japan Meteorological Agency (JMA) upgrades the system to a tropical storm, naming it Haiyan.

5 November Haiyan is reclassified as a typhoon when winds increase to 120 km per hour. It is forecasted to make landfall in the Philippines.

6 November Typhoon Haiyan pounds Palau with sustained winds up to 295 km per hour. The JMA again upgrades Haiyan, this time to a super typhoon, stronger than a category five hurricane. Super Typhoon Haiyan continues to move westwards, swelling to more than 800 km in diameter.

7 November Super Typhoon Haiyan intensifies again before it enters the Philippine region, where it is referred to as Super Typhoon Yolanda.

8 November 04:40 PST (Philippine Standard Time) Super Typhoon Yolanda makes initial landfall in the Philippines at the city of Guiuan on the island of Samar in the Eastern Visayas region. With maximum sustained winds of up to 314 km per hour, it is described as the strongest tropical storm to make landfall at peak strength in recorded world history.

08:00 PST (approx.) Super Typhoon Yolanda slams eastern Samar and Leyte. Tacloban City, with a population of 220 000, bears the full force of winds in excess of 298 km per hour and violent storm surges up to approximately 5 m. Tacloban City and coastal barangays are flattened, power and communications are cut, roads are blocked and air and sea ports suffer severe damage.

By late afternoon, Super Typhoon Yolanda's eye is over northern Panay, central Philippines. Later in the evening it moves into the South China Sea as winds reduce to less than 233 km per hour. Super Typhoon Yolanda is reclassified as a typhoon.

10 November Super Typhoon Yolanda further weakens, making landfall in north-east Vietnam, eventually dissipating over Guangxi in southern China.

The Philippines' National Disaster
Risk Reduction and Management Council
(NDRRMC) confirms at least 1774 deaths,
mainly in the Eastern Visayas.

11 November President Benigno Aquino III
declares a state of national calamity. In
Tacloban City 24 000 family food packs are
distributed, while 18.7 billion Philippine
pesos (PHP) is allocated for emergency
relief. Twenty-two foreign countries
including the United States, Australia,
Canada and Japan pledge millions of dollars
in humanitarian aid as international TV
crews continue to arrive in the country.

The Philippine National Police deploy
883 personnel, including Special Action
Forces, to Tacloban City, and the rest of the
Eastern Visayas. The government responds
to reports of looting by deploying police
reinforcements and a 500-member military
battalion. The devastated Tacloban airport
is set up as an aid hub with a makeshift
hospital. Hundreds of Taclobanons line
up at the airport hoping to secure passage
on the military cargo planes that begin the
relief effort.

12 November The United Nations (UN)
releases US$20 million in emergency funds

as the USS *George Washington* aircraft carrier with 5000 crew heads to the region to desalinate water. The UN and the Department of Foreign Affairs launch an action plan to rehabilitate the 40-plus affected provinces. In Tacloban City, the government sends in armoured vehicles, sets up checkpoints and imposes a curfew to help curtail looting.

The crippled Tacloban City airport struggles to accommodate large cargo planes although some military helicopters begin ferrying water and food. The response is severely hampered by lack of infrastructure and fuel, and government logistical issues.

13 November International news agencies report the government's response efforts have been slow and delayed. Streams of evacuees and road damage hinder aid trucks entering the city. Damage in outlying regions is unable to be assessed.

Japan donates US$10 million in aid and sends relief troops. A civilian medical team arrives from Australia and Australia upgrades its donation to AUD$30 million.

President Benigno Aquino III commits to the delivery of 50 000 relief packs every few days due to the magnitude of the devastation.

The death toll rises to 2275. More than 9 million people have been affected across a large swath of the country. Ninety per cent of homes in the hardest-hit areas have been destroyed. Relief goods accumulate at airports, and foreign and local medical teams and relief workers are also stranded as outlying areas remain unsupported.

The UN launches a global appeal with US$25 million from the Central Emergency Response Fund being made available. The Royal Australian Air Force arrives at Cebu, delivering a portable field hospital destined for Tacloban City.

14 November The *George Washington* strike group, with six ships and 21 helicopters, arrives in the Eastern Visayas.

Six days after the storm, the inadequate airport clinic is one of the few relief centres. Medical supplies are scant with most people still without water and food. Aid continues to pile up at the airport. International news crews report seeing little evidence of any large-scale organised relief effort. The NDRRMC's official death toll climbs to 2357 with 3853 injured and 77 missing. Of the 40 towns in Leyte, 20 remain without communications.

15 November The NDRRMC reports the death toll is 3621 with 1140 missing and 12 165 injured as millions of people wait for aid to arrive. Initial estimates of damage to agriculture, fisheries and irrigation infrastructure reach more than PHP7 billion. In Tacloban City, 90% of school buildings are damaged.

16 November The UN estimates about 12 million people have been affected as mass-grave burials begin. Total damage costs rise to PHP9.46 billion. The government finally decides to airdrop relief goods to remote barangays.

A Bloomberg report forecasts economic loss to be approximately US$15 billion, making Super Typhoon Yolanda one of the most expensive disasters in Philippine history.

17 November Some relief goods finally reach all 40 towns in Leyte. The president revisits Tacloban City to oversee relief operations. The damage toll exceeds PHP10 billion as the death toll climbs to 3 976 with 18 175 people reported injured and 1 590 missing.

21 November Australia's National Critical Care and Trauma Response Centre sends a team of 37 personnel to relieve the critical response crew based in a 50-bed field hospital at the Tacloban airport. Huge logistical issues continue to surround infrastructure, water sanitation, power and housing, hampering widespread relief efforts, particularly in remote areas.

23 November The official death toll exceeds 5 200. Super Typhoon Yolanda is considered to be the deadliest disaster in Philippine history. Over 14 million people across more than 40 provinces have been affected. Tacloban City suffers the greatest loss of life. Five hundred thousand houses have been destroyed and at least 580 000 have suffered severe damage. More than 1.9 million people are believed to be homeless and more than 6 million displaced. The major rice- and sugar-producing areas of the Philippines have been destroyed.

May 2014 Public access to shelter and water is still limited. Major aid agencies including the International Red Cross continue the relief effort. The NDRRMC estimates approximately 6 000 people have died, and records US$184 million in damages to infrastructure in the Eastern Visayas. Save the Children estimates 4 million children and adults have been displaced.

8 November 2014 The first anniversary of the disaster is commemorated in Tacloban with the planting of 2300 white crosses in memory of those buried in the city and outskirts. Hundreds protest in Tacloban City and in the capital Manila at the lack of reconstruction progress.

Two and a half million people remain in temporary shelters with 100 000 residing in coastal areas officially declared unsafe. In Samar province, only 85 of 634 official evacuation shelters remain intact.

2015 Thousands of Filipinos continue to live in temporary shelters or tent cities with inadequate services and employment opportunities despite the government's 'Build Back Better' initiative. According to the economic planning secretary, recovery and reconstruction efforts continue to be hampered by implementation bottlenecks, contradictory policies and bureaucratic weaknesses.

2016 Tacloban's iconic Santo Niño Church has been repaired and a substantial relocation program is underway to rehouse coastal dwellers in safer areas in the north of the city, but tens of thousands of Taclobanons continue to live in areas designated as 'no dwelling zones'. Vice President Leni Robredo admits that only about 1% of the 205 000 homes pledged have been constructed. Water supply remains a problem but plans are underway to expedite supply to Tacloban's relocated township.

Taclobanons' livelihoods are severely compromised as employment opportunities are scarce in the new communities and people have resorted to traditional occupations that offer very little return.

2017 President Rodrigo Duterte orders government offices to complete the transfer of 14 433 Yolanda-hit families out of coastal communities and into resettlement sites with permanent housing by March.

2017–2018 The Eastern Visayas has shown significant growth but is still one of the poorest regions in the Philippines. Communities attend disaster risk–reduction training sessions and community evacuation drills led by NGOs such as Save the Children in an effort to increase resilience and preparedness in the face of impending disasters.

Glossary

anak ko little one

ayo come on

baduya nga pasayan shrimp fritters

bangka boat

banig mat

bantay guard, a common name for dogs in the
Philippines

barangay neighbourhood; the smallest administrative
division in the Philippines

Basta ang Waray, hindi uurong sa away 'Waray
people never back down from a fight' – a popular
saying

corioso butter cookies

idoy young man

jeepney small bus or truck with a long bench down
each side for passengers

kuya big brother

lumpia Filipino spring roll

mano sir

marasa delicious

maupay nga gab-i good evening

padayon an kinabuhi life goes on

pancit noodles

pangaon kita let's eat

peso Philippine currency

pulisya police

salamat thank you

swerte good luck

taklub basket trap used to catch fish and shellfish

trumpo spinning top toy

waray sapayan you're welcome

Waray-waray regional language spoken in Tacloban and Samar

Find out more about...

Super Typhoon Haiyan/Yolanda
https://youtube.com
Search for 'Tacloban before and after Typhoon Yolanda'
(Warning: contains distressing footage)

https//www.britannica.com
Search for 'Super Typhoon Haiyan'

www.bbc.com
Search for 'Typhoon Haiyan: Before and after the storm'

www.abc.net.au
Search for 'The World Today: Survivors describe scenes that are "worse than hell"'

International relief effort
www.abc.net.au
Search for 'Typhoon Haiyan: Field hospital'

https://youtube.com
Search for 'International medical teams aid Haiyan victims'

Recovery and reconstruction
www.caritas.org.au/haiyan

www.irinnews.org
Search for 'Philippines has built only 1% of homes promised after Typhoon Haiyan'

www.youtube.com
Search for 'Tacloban Philippines'

Acknowledgements

With thanks to Sol Vanzi who bravely worked with our crew during our time in Tacloban City and generously advised me on cultural and language aspects of this manuscript. Thank you to cameraman David Leland who worked tirelessly with me covering the typhoon under difficult circumstances, and colleagues Stephen McDonell and Wayne McAllister who flew in to provide backup.

My deepest admiration goes to the people of Tacloban City who remained so strong in the face of such devastation. I will never forget your strength of character.

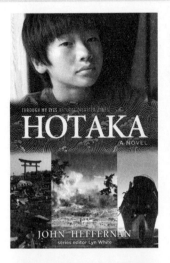
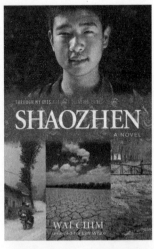